First published in Great Britain by HarperCollins *Children's Books* 2010
HarperCollins *Children's Books* is a division of HarperCollins*Publishers* Ltd,
77-85 Fulham Palace Road, Hammersmith, London W6 8JB

The HarperCollins website is
www.harpercollins.co.uk

1

THE FAMILIARS: Animal Wizardry
Text copyright © Adam Epstein and Andrew Jacobson 2010
Illustrations copyright © Cherie Zamazing 2010

The authors asserts the moral right to be identified as the authors of this work.

ISBN-13 978-0-00-737177-8

Printed and bound in England by
Clays Ltd, St Ives plc

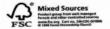

THE FAMILIARS

ANIMAL WIZARDRY

Adam Jay Epstein & Andrew Jacobson

HarperCollins *Children's Books*

For Jane, my wife, who supports and encourages every dream,

no matter how fantastic

For Penny, my daughter, this story is for you

A.J.E.

For Ashley and my familiar, Elvis

A.J.

CONTENTS

ONE

Catch of the Day

It all started with Aldwyn's whiskers beginning to tingle – the way they always did when he got hungry. Food had been getting tougher to come by these last few months. The back alleys weren't littered with their usual fish guts or chicken gizzards, and a stray cat had to fight a little harder to get even one full meal a day.

The whisker-tingling began early one morning, when Aldwyn sat perched atop a shingle rooftop, casually taking in the scenery. His mangy coat of black and white fur looked as if it had never been washed – which was more or less true. The tip of his left ear was missing; a bite-sized reminder of a skirmish with an angry pit bull terrier from when he was a kitten.

Looking out, Aldwyn could see all of Bridgetower. There were rows upon rows of two-storey stone buildings along the narrow cobbled streets. Robed city custodians were hurrying to finish their pre-dawn chores: one used a bell-shaped snuffer to extinguish the candles in the waist-high lamp posts lining the city's darker alleyways; another laid down straw on the main street to quieten the *click-clacking* of the mules' hooves that would soon be pulling rattling wagons along the roadways. Aldwyn's eyes were drawn to the spired watchtower of polished white marble that stood higher than the rest of the skyline. Its guardpost had been empty for over half a century, ever since the brave and noble wizard, Queen Loranella, helped fight back the Dead Army Uprising. A flag billowed at the very top of the watchtower, bearing the Bridgetower coat of arms: a double-headed eagle, holding a bow and arrow in one talon and a wand in the other.

Aldwyn could see beyond the white walls that encircled the city as well: to the west, the Ebs River; to the east, the Aridifian Plains and the forests of the queendom. But he had never set foot outside Bridgetower, and he never intended to, comfortable on the city streets he knew so well.

With dawn's first ray of light, a morning bell chimed brightly, waking Aldwyn from his daydream. He turned his attention to the back door of the local fish and fowl shop, waiting patiently for the fishmonger to appear with the catch of the day. Stealing was one of Aldwyn's favourite schemes to fill his belly, but he used many others. Just last night, he found himself acting – cooing like a pigeon to get bits of cheese from a blind lady feeding birds in the park.

Sure enough, right on schedule yet again, there was the fishmonger, carrying a heavy, dripping burlap bag towards his store. And even though Aldwyn couldn't see what was inside the bag, he could smell it: river flounder! As the old man closed the door to his shop behind him, Aldwyn started counting the toes on his paw.

One... two... three... four.

Like every morning at this precise time, the fishmonger opened the window, airing out the kitchen as he dumped the fish into a bucket beside him. Now Aldwyn could begin his descent from the rooftop. He climbed down the wall, his claws leaving scratch marks on the stone. He crossed the alley, darting around puddles from last night's rain. A short-eared raccoon limped out from behind the corner, trying to keep his weight off an injured hind leg.

"Morning, Aldwyn," said the raccoon. "Heard the afternoon milk wagon is taking a detour tomorrow to avoid the Shield Festival. It's going to be heading through Hangman's Square instead."

"Thanks for the tip," Aldwyn called back. "I'll try to push a jug off the back of the cart when it rounds the Glyphstone. Make sure you're there for lick up."

Aldwyn had made a habit of thinking three meals ahead. He relied on everything from careful observation to back-alley alliances. Finding food was a full-time job — and an exhausting one at that. A freak hailstorm had struck in the middle of the summer, wiping out most of Bridgetower's typically plentiful harvest. Hungry townsfolk were making use of the tripe and offal they once threw away.

The raccoon gave an appreciative nod, and Aldwyn quickly returned to the task at hand. After jumping onto the crates stacked up outside the fishmonger's window, he waited, watching the old man clean and gut the flounder. Aldwyn was nothing if not patient; he knew from experience that there would be a moment when the fishmonger got distracted. An early customer knocking at the front door, a trip to the outhouse, or a dull blade in need of sharpening would give Aldwyn the opportunity he needed to strike.

"Get up here, there's a spider on the bed!" hollered a shrill voice from the top of the stairs.

So today it was his wife. The fishmonger set down his knife and hurried from the kitchen.

"I'm coming," he called.

Aldwyn didn't hesitate. As soon as the old man was out of view, he leaped to the windowsill and slipped through. Once inside the kitchen, he quickly took in the mess of wooden chopping blocks, knives overdue for a cleaning and pewter scales stained with dried fish guts. Then he pounced to the wooden floor below. The overpowering stench of brined eel, which was permanently soaked into the pine floorboards, invaded Aldwyn's nostrils, making his stomach growl with delight. The fishmonger's apron, smeared with dirty handprints, hung on the door handle of the salting closet. It was long overdue for a scrub in the river. The fancier shops on the main square might have kept their counters cleaner, but so what? The flounder here tasted just as good.

Aldwyn moved stealthily to the bucket, grabbing a large flat-fish in his mouth. Soon, he'd be feasting in the privacy of the city's chimney tops, enjoying a nice—

Thwack!

A cat trap snared his tail, missing his neck by a matter of inches. Aldwyn spun around to see a metal coil twist around his fur. He fought the urge to let out an ear-splitting cry, instead burying his whiskers in the back of his right front paw and emitting a muffled whimper. After the initial shock had passed, there was just one question left on his mind: *Since when did the old fishmonger set traps?*

Then things went from bad to worse because out from behind the salting closet emerged the dark, foreboding figure of a man cloaked in black, his face scarred by claw marks. He wore black leather boots with bronze spikes protruding from the toes and carried a crossbow slung over his shoulder. His eyes lit up with cruel delight.

"Gotcha!" said the mysterious figure.

Aldwyn desperately tried to free himself from the rusty metal vice, using his hind legs to push.

"Teach you to steal from me, cat," snarled the fishmonger, popping his head around the corner with a satisfied glint in his eyes.

Aldwyn couldn't believe that he had walked right into an elaborate trap! He, the cleverest alley cat in all of Bridgetower, had let himself be outsmarted? That was only supposed to happen to mice and cockroaches. Not him.

The man in black took a step forwards, pulling out a long wooden pole with a circular rope at the end. At the sight of the dreaded noose stick, Aldwyn's survival instinct kicked in. He leaped for the window. Aldwyn's torso twisted through the open crack, but the metal trap dangling from his tail was too big for the narrow slit. Stuck between inside and outside, Aldwyn glanced back to see the cloaked figure fast approaching. His paws pushed at the window, trying to open it enough to set himself free. The figure reached out to snatch him, but then, at the last second, the window budged another few centimetres, allowing Aldwyn to pull the trap through. He tumbled backwards into the alley, away from the man's grasp.

Aldwyn landed on his feet – one of the advantages of being a cat – and took off running. The metal trap dragged behind him. Out of the corner of his eye, he could see the fishmonger emerge alongside his scar-faced accomplice at the window.

"He's getting away!" hollered the fishmonger.

"Well, he won't get far," responded the man with the bronze-tipped boots, not looking the least bit concerned.

Aldwyn sprinted down the alley, sparks flying as the metal scraped against the cobblestones, fighting hard to keep his balance. He had been chased before, but never with a trap stuck to his tail like a very angry crab. Usually Aldwyn would have made a dash for the rooftops to get away, but he couldn't, not with this thing weighing him down. He glanced back to see his pursuer exit the fish and fowl shop, pulling his crossbow from his side.

Still carrying the fish in his mouth, Aldwyn darted between two buildings and found a hiding place in a pile of scraps discarded by the neighbouring swordsmith. He dug his way in, then crouched very still.

"Hey, whiskers, what's the big idea?" asked a voice from behind him.

Aldwyn turned to see a skinny rat gnawing on a piece of mouldy bread with several of his rodent friends. With the fish between his teeth, Aldwyn whispered, "Gentlemen, nice to see you all again. Don't mind me. Just passing through."

"Oh, no you don't," said the skinny rat, now recognising Aldwyn. "Last time you said that, you brought a knife-wielding butcher into our scrap heap."

"Which we can all agree was really quite funny when you think about it," said Aldwyn with a chuckle. "Right?"

The rats just stared back at him coldly, none too amused.

17

"I can tell this is a sore subject. But I'm more than willing to let bygones be bygones if you are."

One of the other rodents, short and stout with curly whiskers, looked down and saw the cat trap around Aldwyn's tail. "You're in some kind of trouble, aren't you?"

"What, this?" replied Aldwyn, pointing to the metal snare. "It's the latest fashion. They come in three different shades of rust."

The skinny rat poked his head round the corner, then darted back with panic in his eyes.

"It's Grimslade!"

And suddenly Aldwyn knew that he really was in trouble: Grimslade was the infamous bounty hunter. Flyers plastered around the city advertised his services to kill any pest or vermin in exchange for a bounty, to be paid in gold coins or jewels. Grimslade loved his job. Especially when he got to hunt cats. Rumour had it that his distaste for felines went back to his childhood, when his mother paid more attention to her five Abyssinian shorthairs than to him. While his mother's aristocratic pedigree cats had been allowed to curl up in the warmth of a bed each night, young

Grimslade was forced to sleep on the cellar floor. Those early years of neglect had turned him into a bounty hunter: the vindictive, ruthless killer of all creatures who walked on four, six or eight legs, that he was today. Yes, Grimslade was what was commonly known as *extremely bad news*. And he was stalking Aldwyn through the streets of Bridgetower. Aldwyn tried to keep his cool, but there was real fear in his eyes now.

Together, the rats began pushing Aldwyn out from their hideaway.

"All right, so long," said the skinny rat. "Bye-bye now."

"Wait," said Aldwyn, pretending to be a friend. "From one furry animal brother to another, please help me out. You know I would do the same for you."

Without a moment's hesitation, the rats shoved Aldwyn back into the open, right into Grimslade's line of sight. The bounty hunter took aim, firing off his crossbow and sending a bolt whizzing past Aldwyn's shoulder.

Word had travelled across the rooftops that Grimslade kept a collection of paws from his previous bounties and Aldwyn did not want to become part of his trophy case. As Grimslade pulled back the mechanism for a second shot, Aldwyn darted for cover behind one of the lamp posts. Grimslade's arrow shattered the glass bowl housing the candle above Aldwyn's head, sending a shower of still-warm wax onto the ground. Aldwyn stood there panting, pondering his next move. Then he heard the sound of metal smashing against metal, and he had an idea. He took off running for the nearby swordsmith's workshop.

In the soot-covered and smoke-filled smithy, a large man was hammering flat a broadsword, the kind used by the queen's soldiers when they patrolled the streets for pickpockets and vandals. The swordsmith, protected from the embers that were leaping from the hearth by nothing more than a leather apron, was covered in sweat from the heat of the dancing flames. He kept pounding away at the sword, sending tiny bursts of blue sparks from the anvil into the air. Aldwyn leaped for the ironwork table, carefully positioning the trap directly between the falling hammer and the sword. With a loud clang, the hammer came down square on the metal trap, splitting it in half, allowing Aldwyn to slip his tail free. He made a mental note to add this to his list of greatest escapes, then bolted out through a side door before the swordsmith could even realise what he had done.

Finally trap-free and back at full speed, Aldwyn's feet barely touched the ground. He ran through the copper district, where merchants were busy setting up displays of hand-crafted candlesticks and cooking vats outside their shop fronts. But Grimslade emerged once more, not to be denied his prize. This was, after all, the same man who was said to have burned an entire building to the ground just to root out a single 'roach. When Aldwyn looked back, he was emboldened by the growing distance between him and his pursuer, but he wasn't going to take any chances. He kept running at full speed. The next time he looked back, he saw that Grimslade had done something unexpected: he had stopped dead in his tracks. He loosened the gold drawstrings of a leather pouch hanging from his belt and a shadowy puff of smoke burst out, quickly assuming the shape of a dog. Aldwyn tried hard not to panic, because just as tales of Grimslade's villainous doings had spread through the back alleys, so too had stories of his shadow hounds. Concocted from black magic, these canine apparitions were conjured from a mix of onyx, black mondo grass and burned lupine hair. The tongueless cave shamans from Stalagmos who brewed these predatory demons found they could fetch a rich purse in the Sewer Markets from assassins like Grimslade. And they were well worth the coin. First created to guard the pitch-black jasper mines of Udula, shadow hounds could see in the complete absence of light and their teeth could cut through chain mail. It was enough to make any feline fugitive's paws tremble. Aldwyn was beginning to wonder if the fresh and juicy flounder he still held in his mouth was really worth the trouble.

The shadow hound sped towards him, avoiding the beams of morning light. It let out a supernatural growl that made the fur on the back of Aldwyn's neck stand up on end. Picking up the pace, Aldwyn headed straight for what appeared to be a dead end: a fifteen-foot fence that surrounded the sacred rock gardens of Bridgetower's Sun Temple. With the shadow hound closing the gap, Aldwyn got a better look at the beast chasing after him. No eyes, no nose, just a cloud of black that left wisps of smoke in its wake.

Aldwyn hit the wooden planks of the fence running, his claws vaulting him fifteen feet and over. He landed in the rock garden on the other side, confident that no dog would be able to scale the same height. But the shadow hound was no ordinary dog. It moved straight through the fence like vapour, reforming again on the other side. Aldwyn's eyes widened as he took off once more, heading for the front steps to the Sun Temple. Not taking time to admire it more closely, he dashed through the entrance to save his skin.

Inside the temple, citizens of Bridgetower had come to pray for the sun to heal their ruined fields, kneeling before a meditation pool illuminated by rotating mirrors. Rays of morning sunlight shot through a hole in the domed ceiling, bouncing off the glass reflectors and causing the water to glow brightly

Aldwyn passed between two bronze offering bowls filled with flower petals and shiny coins. Overhead grand pictures in gold leaf showed a bearded warrior on a horse pulling the sun across the sky. Aldwyn hoped to run through the temple and sneak out the other side, but found that the silver exit doors had yet to be opened. He turned back to the entrance, only to see the shadow hound blocking his escape. The pads of his paws began to sweat.

"Maybe we can discuss this," pleaded Aldwyn, dropping the flounder to the ground. "What do you say we go halfsies on this fish? Fifty–fifty."

The shadowy apparition snarled ferociously sending tentacles of mist towards Aldwyn. He felt a terrible cold as the mist enveloped his white paw, but the tentacles retreated as quickly as they came.

"Sixty–forty works too," said Aldwyn.

A few of the worshippers looked up from their prayer as the dog moved into the attack position. Baring its jet-black fangs, the hound leaped forwards, flying through the air, straight for Aldwyn's neck. Aldwyn dodged out of the way, finding himself cornered up against one of the large rotating mirrors. Then he had an idea – an idea that would save his life. Just as the shadow hound got ready to pounce again, Aldwyn flicked his paw, spinning the sun reflector so the concentrated beam of sunlight was directed right at the smoky beast. The light seared a hole straight through the apparition and it let out a blood-curdling scream. Then, in a flash of black, the hound exploded. Only a sprinkling of powdered onyx was left behind.

Aldwyn took a deep breath, picked up the flounder and exited the temple with an air of supreme cockiness, ignoring the commotion he had caused among the worshippers. He crossed through the garden, climbed up a nearby tree and leaped over the fence to the neighbouring city street.

Crossing the merchants' square, Aldwyn passed an elderly woman with a patch of chin fuzz selling potted plants from her handcart. He looked around and realised that he had never been along this section before. At first glance, it looked no different from any other row of stalls selling cauldrons, spices or books. But he had never seen steam pour out of an *empty* cauldron, or the pages of books flip *on their own* – although there was a good chance it was just the wind. And, come to think of it, why was the old lady with the chin fuzz selling plants that were shrivelled up and dead? What use could they have? Well, it didn't really matter, as long as there was a flat rooftop where he could finally eat his flounder in peace, and catch a long nap afterwards.

Thwoop!

Aldwyn could feel his teeth vibrating as the fish was shot straight out of his mouth by a bolt from Grimslade's crossbow.

"You're an impressive foe," Grimslade called out. "But the chase ends here."

For a split second, Aldwyn was torn between running for his life and retrieving the fish, which was now pinned to a wooden barrel by the arrow. A second bolt that brushed past the fur on his head helped him make up his mind. Aldwyn dashed around the corner and ran for the first window he could find, leaping into where he did not know.

TWO

Unfamiliar Surroundings

At first he could hardly see anything, so dark was the inside of the room. Then Aldwyn's eyes adjusted to the dimness and he noticed dozens, no, hundreds of open cages, stacked floor to ceiling. Inside were animals of all kinds, from butter newts and salamanders to periwinkle falcons and three-toed sloths. There were spoon-billed mocking birds, badgers and hedgehogs covered in poisonous-looking needles. In a nearby glass tank, six diamond-shelled tortoises levitated in a circle while fast asleep, floating a few inches above the ground. On a shelf beside them, a mouse with a single ivory horn sticking out from its head was in the middle of a heated debate with a hairless aardvark.

"You can't cast a proper hex without black lichen," argued the mouse.

"Yeah, well you'd be surprised what you can do with locust dung," said the aardvark. "It's a pretty versatile component."

"But who wants to smell that stuff?" responded the mouse, cringing.

Aldwyn didn't have the faintest idea what they were talking about – hexes, components, locust dung – so he decided to turn his attention to a neighbouring cage, where a buck-toothed wombat was munching on the last bite of a baby carrot. After finishing, he gave his tiny tail a shake and disappeared. Aldwyn blinked, not sure if the light was playing tricks on his eyes. He gave a quick glance around and spotted the wombat now standing on the shop counter, stuffing her furry pouch with more carrots from a wooden bowl.

It was a lot for Aldwyn to take in, these unusual creatures with their unusual talents. But before he could give it any more thought, he spotted a rotund, middle-aged man with curly red hair walking out from the stock room with a cup of appleberry cider in his hand.

"Hey, you," a voice whispered from behind Aldwyn. "You'd better get back in your cage."

Aldwyn turned and saw that the warning had come from a large-eyed lemur who was hanging upside down in his cage. On second thoughts, it couldn't be a lemur, since as far as Aldwyn knew lemurs definitely did not have two tails.

Aldwyn spotted an empty cage and scurried over towards it. He figured this would be a perfect place to lie low for a little while. Grimslade would never come looking for him in here, and if he did, he wouldn't be able to find him among this bizarre collection of animal oddities. He was probably still combing the back alleys looking for kitty droppings. Aldwyn tried to pull open the handle with his paw, but lacking a thumb made gripping and turning the metal knob a bit of a challenge. As the shopkeeper crossed through the shop, Aldwyn used his teeth and tail to help unclasp the cage door. With a pop, the gate finally swung open and Aldwyn slid inside just as the curly haired man passed by on his way to the counter. A tiny bell over the door rang as two customers and a gust of air swept in from outside. Aldwyn had a clear view to the front of the shop, where a bald, moustached elderly man, dressed in a black robe decorated with tiny stars, was accompanied by a young boy, whose green eyes peeked out from beneath his dirty blond hair. The shopkeeper put down his cup of cider and walked over to greet them.

"Ah, Kalstaff, I've been expecting you," he said before turning to the young boy. "And this must be Jack."

"It is. And it's his birthday," replied Kalstaff. "He turns eleven today."

"Then you've come to the right place. I have the best selection of familiars east of Split River."

Ah, so that explained all the extraordinary creatures in this store: they were *familiars*, the animal companions to wizards and witches or any spellcaster. It was common knowledge that familiars assisted their humans in tasks both remarkable and mundane, but that they possessed magical powers of their own was known only by those who had had a first-hand encounter with a familiar – a select group that Aldwyn was now a part of. He turned his attention back to the boy, who appeared overwhelmed by the choices before him. He'd begun to wander around the shop, peeking into this cage then that.

"How do I choose?" asked Jack.

"That depends on what kind of wizard you wish to become," replied the shopkeeper. "Say you're keen on healing magic. Then perhaps your talents would best be complemented by a raven." He gestured to a black bird sitting on a perch. "Ravens are capable of mending wounds with a stroke of their feathers."

"I want to be a Beyonder," said Jack. "I want to travel to distant lands and fight off enemies. Maybe I'll be the first one to find the centre of Necro's Maze."

"In that case, we can skip past the elephant snails and ponder toads," replied the shopkeeper.

Aldwyn watched Jack head in his direction, with Kalstaff right behind him. As they got closer, he noticed that the stars on Kalstaff's robe were spinning and what had to be a magic rod was floating at his side. Aldwyn had never seen one in the flesh before, but going by the looks of these enchanted items, it was easy to guess that Kalstaff was a wizard; and the boy had to be one of his pupils.

Aldwyn, like everyone, knew that spellcasters walked among the non-magical majority of Vastia's population. Often indistinguishable from regular folk, magicians lived peacefully alongside those that didn't have the gift, serving as teachers and healers and protectors of the queendom in times of peril. At least that's what Aldwyn once overheard two town elders discussing while he was hiding under a loose floorboard in an all-you-can-eat sausage parlour. Not that he'd been paying close attention – he'd been rather distracted by a puddle of pork grease that had dripped to the floor beside the buffet table.

Jack pointed to a snake-like creature with little wings on its back.

"What's this?"

"That's a pocket dragon. They can breathe fire."

Aldwyn watched with a sense of wonder as wisps of flame shot out from the pocket dragon's nostrils.

"But they also have a tendency to burn your hair off," continued the shopkeeper. "I don't recommend them, unless you want to be as bald as Kalstaff."

While burning your hair off might be an unpleasant side effect to a human, it was downright terrifying to a cat. Aldwyn would be keeping his distance from pocket dragons.

"This is one of my personal favourites," said the shopkeeper as they passed a brass pot with a small crab sitting in a pool of water. "Chameleon crabs. They specialise in camouflage spells that can make themselves and their loyals blend in with their surroundings."

Loyals? Aldwyn had never heard the word used in this way before. But it was clear that the shopkeeper was referring to a familiar's human companion.

The shopkeeper dipped his hand into the pot for a demonstration and within seconds his skin began to change colour, starting with his feet turning the same dark brown as the floor. Then his legs and torso transformed into the metallic grey of the cage doors behind him. Before he was entirely camouflaged, he pulled his hand out of the bowl and immediately returned to his normal state.

The boy stood with a look of awe on his face.

"I just don't know," said Jack, clearly torn between too many options. "They're all so amazing."

"Yes, they are," said the shopkeeper with great respect. "But count yourself fortunate. There was a time when young wizards-in-training didn't have so many choices, when they had to go and find their familiar out in the wild. That's why my great-grandfather opened this store. To make certain that spellcasters would get the best assistance the animal kingdom could offer."

"It was at this very shop that I chose Zabulon as a boy," said Kalstaff. "And the queen found her familiar, Paksahara."

Jack turned and spied a six-inch long green lizard wearing a tiny saddle on its back, peering out from between two candlesticks on the counter. The shopkeeper came up behind the boy. "That's a riding lizard."

"For what? Ants?"

"No, for people," answered the store owner. "Rub the back of its head."

Jack stood there reluctantly at first. Then curiosity got the better of him. He reached his hand out and ran his finger across the lizard's scaly scalp. The diminutive reptile flicked out its tongue, striking the boy's fingernail and causing him to shrink to the size of a peanut and land on the lizard's back. He fitted perfectly in the miniature riding gear.

"Hey, what happened?" squeaked Jack, who had to grab onto the reins for dear life as the riding lizard sprinted down the counter, leaping over ink pots and feeding dishes. Jack managed to brace his now minuscule feet in the stirrups as the galloping reptile charged for the edge of the counter, racing straight past Aldwyn, who watched from inside his cage.

As the lizard sped towards the three-foot drop, the inch-tall Jack seemed half terrified and half thrilled, his hair bouncing in and out of his eyes. Then the two went airborne and the shopkeeper snatched the lizard out from under the boy. As soon as Jack was no longer touching the magic reptile, he expanded back to his normal size and landed with a thud on the floor.

"I think I'm going to pass on that one," said Jack, shaking off the after effects of the spell before dizzily rising to his feet. He was starting to look a little discouraged.

"Just remember Pharkum's three T's of animal companionship. Temperament, Toughness and Talent," advised the shopkeeper. "At least two should match your own."

Kalstaff put a reassuring hand on the young boy's shoulder.

"But what's most important is that you find a connection with your familiar," he said. "Its magic skills won't help you, however impressive they may be, unless you share this deep bond. You'll know when you feel it."

The shopkeeper gestured to the cage before Aldwyn's, with the large-eyed lemur – or whatever it was – still hanging upside down.

"This one came from the jungles north of Vastia. It can see through solid objects. Nifty talent, but impossible to get any privacy."

Jack only half heard, as he had already moved on to Aldwyn. The boy bent down and looked straight into his eyes. Aldwyn was attempting to lie low and not call any attention to himself, but here he was being singled out. He tried to look bored and as uninteresting as possible.

"This cat's got green eyes, just like me," said Jack.

The shopkeeper walked over and looked at Aldwyn.

"I don't remember where I got that one. Must have been one of the telekinetic bicolours I picked up from Maidenmere."

"Ooh, I want to see!" exclaimed the boy.

They all waited expectantly, but Aldwyn just lay there.

"The truly powerful don't need to put their talents on display," said the shopkeeper. "His gifts must be especially strong."

Aldwyn couldn't believe just how mistaken the store owner was. He was an ordinary alley cat, whose only real talent was for getting into trouble.

"I'll take him," Jack blurted out.

Aldwyn thought he hadn't heard right. Had the young wizard apprentice, in this shop filled with countless amazing animals, each one more magical than the next, really picked him as his familiar?

"Are you sure?" asked the shopkeeper. "This is not like a wand or a hat. A familiar must be chosen very carefully."

Jack reached into the cage and stroked the underside of Aldwyn's chin with the backs of his fingers. Aldwyn instinctively nuzzled his cheek against the boy's hand and a little purr of pleasure escaped from his mouth. He felt his tail curl, something that rarely happened. He didn't know why, but Aldwyn felt a connection to Jack, an instant sense of belonging that could only be described as magical.

A smile crossed Kalstaff's face. "He's sure."

The bald wizard handed the shopkeeper a leather purse filled with coins and Jack pulled Aldwyn out into his arms.

"I'm going to name him Mittens!" he said excitedly to Kalstaff. Aldwyn shuddered at the thought.

"This is no ordinary pet," replied the old wizard. "You don't name them. Familiars reveal their names to you."

"But how?" asked the boy.

"*Vocarum Animale*, a simple but powerful spell created by Horteus Ebekenezer, the great forest communer. You'll see later."

Before they reached the door, the shopkeeper called out to Jack with one last piece of advice.

"Don't expect too much from him at first," he said. "He will reveal his powers when the time is right."

With Aldwyn in his arms, Jack nodded and followed Kalstaff back out onto the street. Aldwyn spied Grimslade lingering on the corner, his crossbow poised menacingly in hand. A most distressing image flashed through Aldwyn's mind: his own fur laid out on Grimslade's sitting-room floor as a catskin rug. Quickly, Aldwyn nestled deeper into Jack's arms, hoping he would remain hidden and out of sight.

"Let's pick up some fish for your new friend before heading home," suggested Kalstaff.

Aldwyn felt his whiskers tingling and couldn't hold back another happy purr. It had been a rough start to the day, but at long last things were looking up.

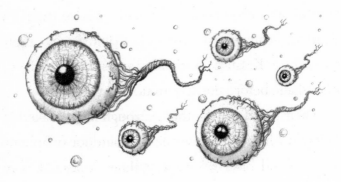

THREE

Stone Runlet

As promised, before leaving Bridgetower Aldwyn had enjoyed a delectable piece of fresh fish. Then, tucked in the crook of Jack's arm, he'd been carried across the wide stone overpass built above the moat that surrounded the easternmost wall of the city. Upon reaching the other side, the old wizard led them along a dirt road that wound its way towards the highlands. It wasn't long before they passed a caravan of driftfolk, tattooed travelling merchants selling beads and spices out of the back of their mule-drawn wagons. As the driftfolk crowded around the trio, Aldwyn caught a whiff of orange-mint and cumin clinging to their garments. Kalstaff purchased a small pinch of nightshade before they continued on their way.

Their journey took them through hills cloaked in emerald whistlegrass humming an outdoor symphony as the wind blew over the rolling slopes. Aldwyn listened as Kalstaff told Jack how every field had its own song. Each told a different story, some playing triumphant marches in honour of battles fought there long ago, others whispering lullabies for those who had slept soundly under the starlight.

They left the whistlegrass behind them, and, having veered off the main road, made their way across the Aridifian Plains, an expanse of rock and sand where what little vegetation remained had been singed black. Aldwyn quickly spotted the reason why: volcano ants! These bright red insects had built thousands of anthills, with tunnels that stretched down to the earth's very core. The magma that spat out from the tiny hills had charred everything green in its path and a traveller had to be extra careful not to set their boots on fire while stepping through these parts.

Aldwyn thought himself a fairly knowledgeable cat, but he was already realising just how little he knew of the natural wonders that lay outside Bridgetower's walls.

The last hour of the trip had been nothing but field after field of half-harvested crops. The barley stalks hung limply, a result of the sudden hail of snow and ice that had fallen on that otherwise warm summer day. During the long walk back home, Kalstaff and Jack had only taken a short rest to shake the sand out of their leather boots. Now, as the sun was setting, they were crossing a tiny stream and heading for an isolated meadow whose name, Stone Runlet, was written on a signpost.

Stepping out of the runlet's ankle-deep water, they entered the low-lying field. Up ahead, Aldwyn spotted a small stone cottage on the edge of a wood. Fruit trees, berry trees and oak trees with leaves the size of pie crusts lined the glen. A boy around the age of fourteen with a square jaw and broad shoulders sat under one of the trees reading an oversized book bound in a beautiful leather binding. Above him, a girl, who also appeared to be about fourteen, sat on a thick branch juggling three walnuts. Ringlets of blonde hair were falling over her face.

"Marianne, Dalton, we're back!" Jack called out.

The girl swung down from the tree, making a perfect landing on the ground below. The boy carefully marked his page before closing the book, then stood up. The two walked over to welcome the returning travellers.

Aldwyn could now see that both the boy and the girl were accompanied by animal companions of their own. A blue jay sat on Dalton's shoulder, its feathers a deeper shade of blue than the sky itself. Marianne was joined by a red-eyed swamp frog, its bright orange feet clinging to her cloak. Aldwyn couldn't help but wonder what special powers these two familiars possessed.

"Let me see," said Marianne as she ran up to Jack. "What did you get?"

"A cat. And his eyes are the same colour as mine. He's still got his claws, too. I bet he could do a lot of damage in a fight."

Aldwyn was jolted from his comfortable resting

position as Jack, in a burst of excitement, thrust him out for the older kids to see.

"He's a little skinny," said Dalton. "But so are you."

"Am not."

Dalton ruffled Jack's hair, then turned to the blue jay. "What do you think, Skylar?" he asked.

Hold on, thought Aldwyn – did the boy, Dalton, expect a *bird* to answer his question? How bizarre was that? Aldwyn had always been able to understand humans, but as far as he knew no human had ever understood him.

Skylar whispered something back into Dalton's ear, and the boy chuckled to himself.

"That's not fair," said Jack. "What did she say?"

"That your cat looks like he needs a bath."

"Another thing you two have in common," joked Marianne to Jack.

"Very funny, sis," replied Jack, who tucked Aldwyn back under his arm.

"Come along," said Kalstaff. "We've had a long day. Let's have some supper and get an early night."

Dalton and Marianne turned back to the cottage. Jack sighed, looking disappointed.

"Already? But I haven't even shown him how I can levitate stones over the pond with a hover spell. Or taught him how to cast a smoke burst."

"There will be plenty of time to show off your skills tomorrow," said Kalstaff. "But remember, familiars are only meant to use their natural animal talents. Casting human spells is frowned upon. It's much too dangerous for them."

Jack reluctantly put Aldwyn down and sulked off, following Kalstaff and the two older wizards-in-training to the cottage. But Marianne's frog and Dalton's blue jay lingered, curious to meet the newest resident of Stone Runlet. The bird carried herself with a certain aloofness, back straight and beak held high. Her feathers were exquisitely unruffled and she wore a jewelled anklet. The frog had big bulging eyes that gave the impression that he was in a constant state of surprise. The suction pads on his toes made wet blurping sounds with every step. As Aldwyn approached them, the blue jay got a closer look at his fur.

"Are those fleas?" she asked.

Aldwyn glanced down at the tiny black specks on his white patches.

"What? No, those are freckles," he responded.

"Then why are they moving?" she asked as one of the specks jumped off his fur.

Aldwyn quickly brushed them away before extending a paw.

"I'm Aldwyn," he said, eager to change the topic.

The blue jay reluctantly put out her wing for a shake.

"I'm Skylar," she said. "And this is Gilbert."

"But you can call me Gil, or Bert. Gilbert is fine, too," said the frog eagerly. "Do I have any flies in my teeth?"

Gilbert opened his mouth for the others to see. Skylar simply rolled her eyes and continued.

"Well, if you're serious about being a great familiar, there's no better place to learn than here," said Skylar with a hint of pride in her voice. "Of course, some would make an argument for Turnbuckle Academy, or possibly studying with Sorceress Edna, but I just don't…"

Though Skylar kept talking, Aldwyn's mind had wandered. He was thinking about Grimslade and how the cold-blooded bounty hunter was probably still scouring the streets of Bridgetower looking for him. One thing was certain: he'd never look for him here.

After letting this pleasant thought roll around in his head for a minute or two, Aldwyn turned his attention back to the conversation.

"...and Kalstaff has a spell library that would rival any in the queendom," Skylar was saying, still not having come up for air. "He's a master sorcerer, skilled in multiple circles of magic. Necromancy, conjuring, abjuration."

"And he makes a tasty beetle soup," said Gilbert. Skylar just shook her head at him.

"What? That's important too," Gilbert added defensively

Skylar shrugged and turned back to Aldwyn, who was doing his best to hide the fact that he had no idea what she was talking about. "Kalstaff was one of the three great spellcasters who helped defeat the Dead Army Uprising, but that's common knowledge. Which legendary battle is your favourite? Kalstaff was in all of them, you know."

"Gosh, there are so many to choose from," said Aldwyn, trying to stall. Skylar waited for a response.

"But if I had to pick, it would probably be the one where he used the magic…" She continued to stare at him. "…to defeat that scary thing…" Still staring. "…on the mountain."

Her attitude changed instantly. "Oh, the Clash of Kailasa," she enthused. "A little-known engagement, but noteworthy for his use of weevil dust."

"My thoughts exactly," said Aldwyn.

Just then, Gilbert's tongue shot out from his mouth and plucked a juicy horsefly right off Aldwyn's tail. He swallowed it whole, then looked up guiltily.

"I hope you weren't going to eat that."

"Nah, it's all yours," replied Aldwyn.

"Don't mind him," said Skylar. "He's amphibiously challenged. Now where was I? Oh, yes. I was telling you how lucky you were to be here. Kalstaff's students go on to do great things: serve her glorious majesty Loranella, become temple masters, or explore the Beyond in search of new frontiers. And their familiars are always at their sides, aiding their loyals in any way they can. The last student, Galleon, graduated from here a few years ago. He and his familiar, Banshee, have been defending the town of Split River from sea monsters and elven pirates ever since. Very heady stuff."

The prospect of having to fight sea monsters and elven pirates didn't exactly fill Aldwyn with joy, but for the moment, Stone Runlet seemed like paradise – especially given the difficulties he was leaving behind in Bridgetower. Of course, passing himself off as a familiar was not going to be easy, even for a clever alley cat such as himself.

Skylar looked over to see smoke beginning to pour out of the cottage's chimney.

"Gilbert, let's see if we can't be of assistance," added Skylar. "Aldwyn, you might want to wash yourself off down by the runlet first. See if you can't do something about those *freckles*."

With that, she beat her wings and flew off towards the cottage to catch up with Dalton.

"Is she always like that?" asked Aldwyn.

"No," said Gilbert. "Today she's positively cheerful." He put a webbed foot on Aldwyn's paw. "But she's not all bad. Get past the high-and-mighty, know-it-all attitude, and you find a bird that will always watch your back."

"So, what's for dinner?" asked Aldwyn, whose whiskers were once again all a-tingle.

"I like the way you think. I have a feeling we're going to be good friends."

"Hurry up, Gilbert!" called Skylar from the open doorway to the cottage. "You're going to let in the wind fairies."

"I just try to block out the sound of her voice," said Gilbert. "It makes the day go by a lot faster."

Gilbert hopped ahead, but Aldwyn hesitated. Although the prospect of a dip in the runlet sounded most disagreeable, it seemed unwise to ruffle Skylar's feathers.

"Aren't you coming?" asked Gilbert.

"You go ahead," said Aldwyn. "I think maybe I will freshen up after all." Gilbert shrugged and continued towards the cottage.

Aldwyn turned back towards the runlet, which split the meadow in two. In spite of the absence of the crowded streets and marble towers of Bridgetower, this open and empty place already felt strangely like home to him. He trotted ahead, each step cushioned rather pleasantly by the soft grass beneath his feet. His paws, hardened from a life of pounding the city's cobblestone streets, could get used to this!

Aldwyn reached a shallow part of the runlet where he could sit comfortably on the shore while splashing himself gingerly with the water. He began flicking his paw, sending drops of icy water onto his fur. Then something upstream caught his attention: a school of odd-looking tadpoles. Aldwyn rose up on his hind legs to take a closer look at the unusual swarm of baby amphibians. They had white, egg-shaped bodies with veins of red streaking through them. As the tadpoles passed by, something strange happened: they seemed to slow down and stare right at him. That's when Aldwyn realised that these were not tadpoles: they were a pack of swimming eyeballs. Their detached optic nerves wiggled through the water behind them like tiny tails! By the time this shudder-worthy vision had fully registered with Aldwyn, the school of eyes had been taken swiftly downstream by the current.

He had to get another look; his first had been so fleeting he couldn't be sure if what he had seen was really true. Aldwyn hurried along the shore, trying to catch up with the fast-travelling eyeballs. Were they moving freely on their own? Were they the gruesome remains of some hideous crime? Ahead, Aldwyn spied a log that crossed the runlet. If he could reach it in time, he might be able to pounce upon it to get a better glance. He sprinted faster and then took a jump for the length of fallen tree. His claws dug into the wet bark as he steadied himself on the slippery birch. Aldwyn peered down to see the escaping eyes rush past him, under the log and into the light rapids beyond. Aldwyn made a desperate attempt to grab the last of the bobbing and weaving eyeballs, but in his haste took a tumble and found himself neck deep in the freezing runlet. By the time he had waded back to shore, any evidence of his mysterious encounter had disappeared.

On the walk back from the runlet, Aldwyn shook the wet from his fur and gave some thought as to whether or not to speak of this most recent brush with the unbelievable. Would his new companions think him crazy? Best not to find out, he decided. He still wasn't sure how much trust he could place in these strangers. Aldwyn knew from his experiences in Bridgetower that most animals were only out for themselves and he found it hard to believe that these two would be any different.

Aldwyn approached the front door and entered the cottage. It was a quaint dwelling if ever he had seen one. Kalstaff and the young wizards were sitting on vine hammocks strung up to the ceiling in front of a fireplace, eating two-day-old dried mushroom salad. The uneven floor appeared to be made of tree roots woven together; long twisting coils of birch and oak that created a solid surface to stand upon. A collection of antique weapons was mounted on the wall, mostly tarnished swords but also more unusual tools of combat, like a spiked club, a trident and a halberd – trophies from the valiant battles of Kalstaff's past. In the centre of the room hung a hive of twigs and wax, glowing from the lightning bugs that swarmed inside and around it.

Aldwyn poked his nose in a bowl of gizzards that had been left out for him, but an unexpected wave of exhaustion overcame him. For the first time in his life, he was too tired to eat. Which made sense, given all the day's excitement: he had been chased by Grimslade and his demonic shadow hound, seen magical animals in the familiar shop, ventured miles beyond the walls of Bridgetower and discovered that he would be a young wizard's familiar. Not to mention his run-in with the swimming eyeballs. He could only imagine what other surprises were in store for him tomorrow. Suddenly, Aldwyn's eyes became very heavy and before he could even find a cosy place to curl up on the floor, he fell into a deep sleep.

FOUR

Storm Berries and Bookworms

Tiny kitten paws hovered above the grass. It felt as if he was flying... or was he being carried? The sound of a river current came nearer. Then his own face was staring back at him in the water. He was much younger, though, and the tip of his ear was still there. A nest of twigs was floating by. And then he was falling, falling...

Aldwyn awoke from his slumber with a start. He had had this dream before; it visited him on nights of deep, uninterrupted sleep, but its meaning remained a mystery. As he opened his eyes, he had no idea where he was at first. He expected to be surrounded by rooftop shingles and cooing pigeons, but instead found himself on a twisted-root floor in front of a still-crackling fire. Confusion soon gave way to memories of the previous day and its haunting conclusion down by the runlet. There was something foreboding and sinister about the mass of spying eyeballs that made him think he should tell the others about it. But once again, Aldwyn chose to keep the unsettling encounter to himself. He stretched luxuriously and then got up and walked outside, where he was surprised to find the sun hanging high in the sky. When was the last time he had slept this late?

Aldwyn saw that Marianne, Dalton and Jack were already outside the cottage, each holding big, thick volumes of parchment bound by twine in front of them. Kalstaff was waiting for them by a row of tree stumps in the glen, standing in front of a tablet of slate. Aldwyn noticed that it was covered with all kinds of intricate symbols and letters written in chalk. The students sat down in this strange outdoor classroom and Kalstaff began the morning lesson, tapping the glass ball at the tip of his rod against the board three times. A second later, the chalk symbols began to rearrange themselves into an orderly figure of eight.

Aldwyn walked over to Gilbert and Skylar, who waited eagerly nearby to see what assistance the wizards would need during today's tutorial.

"Look at what the cat dragged in," said Skylar, rather stiffly. "That was a joke," she added, seeing Aldwyn's straight-faced reaction. "You know, because you're a cat and you were late."

"She doesn't understand humour," said Gilbert. "See, what she should have said is, 'Talk about a cat nap!'"

Aldwyn let out a laugh. "Now that's funny."

Skylar looked at them, confused. "I don't get it. What's the difference?"

Without answering her question, Gilbert nudged a giant oak leaf towards Aldwyn, who looked down to see a few crumbs of cheese on it.

"I saved you some breakfast," said Gilbert. "But then, umm, I got hungry and ate most of it."

"Why didn't anyone wake me?" asked Aldwyn.

"Kalstaff believes that the natural sleep cycle should

remain undisturbed, that we learn more with our eyes closed than we do with them open," replied Skylar. "Of course, if that were true, Gilbert would be a genius."

"Thank you," said Gilbert cheerfully.

Aldwyn considered telling him it wasn't a compliment, but decided to keep his mouth shut.

Over by the tree stumps, Kalstaff began throwing sprinkles of crushed nightshade into the air.

"Look, Kalstaff is preparing to conjure a fire spirit," whispered Skylar. "We should gather some juniper berries and sage leaves. They'll need them to cast the spell."

With a flap of her wings, Skylar soared off towards the woods. Aldwyn noticed she had a tiny satchel slung across her back.

By the time Aldwyn and Gilbert reached the boundary where the glen met the woods, Skylar was already filling her satchel with ripe, purple berries. Gilbert started plucking sage leaves. Aldwyn pretended to be busy giving his fur another once-over.

"Aldwyn, since it's your first day, I'll leave the basics to you, something even an untrained familiar should be able to handle," said Skylar. "See if you can gather some *Juniperus phoenicea*. I've got the *oxycedrus* covered. Kalstaff says a good blend of varietals creates a more potent invocation."

Aldwyn stared at her like she was speaking a different language. He wouldn't know a juniper berry if it smacked him right on the nose, let alone be able to identify a *Juniperus phoenicea*.

"Sure thing," he said without missing a beat. One thing being an alley cat had taught him was to never admit weakness. "I'll go get the *focaccia*."

"*Phoenicea*."

"Right."

Aldwyn scampered up a neighbouring tree and walked across one of its low-lying branches. He reached out a paw and swiped a few tart yellow berries from the twig. Within the blink of an eye, a grey cloud formed overhead and a small thunderclap could be heard. Skylar and Gilbert both looked over to Aldwyn.

"Why are you picking storm berries?" asked Skylar. Aldwyn thought there was a note of frustration in her voice.

Before he could answer, a shower of rain poured down on the three of them. It only lasted for a few seconds, but it was enough to soak them from head to toe.

"Don't worry about it – I made the same mistake when I first got here," said Gilbert. "I almost got struck by lightning."

Skylar shook the drops of water from her feathers and flew over to a small tree. She began pulling off a slightly darker hued berry with her beak.

"I suppose if you want something done correctly, you have to do it yourself," Skylar said under her breath, but making sure the others could hear. "Elementary education for familiars just isn't what it used to be."

Aldwyn made his way back down to the ground, his damp fur already giving off the musky odour of week-old dish rags. It was evident that he was lacking even the basic knowledge needed to fit in here, but luckily he wasn't expected to know everything about this world… yet. Of course, if he made too many mistakes, he'd be exposed as the magicless, talentless, utterly ordinary cat that he was, and his comfortable new life would be over before it had even begun.

The sky was still a deep purple as dusk slowly turned to night, and the bald wizard ladled second helpings of a homemade stew into Jack and Marianne's wooden bowls. Kalstaff called it dining under the stars. It was a fancy way of saying what Aldwyn did every night back in Bridgetower: eating outdoors.

Aldwyn warmed himself by the fire as he lapped up chunks of fish and potato from a dish of his own. Skylar sat perched on Dalton's forearm, pecking at a pile of nuts and grubs in the palm of his hand. Gilbert was shovelling a bowlful of swamp flies into his mouth. Every so often, he let out a loud belch, barely stopping to take a breath before continuing.

Aldwyn's belly was getting full, but he had worked up quite an appetite during his first official day as a familiar. After accidentally causing the rainstorm while gathering the conjuring ingredients, he had spent the rest of the morning assisting – well, *watching* – Skylar and Gilbert catch the slither of bookworms that had crept into the spell library. Skylar, close to a nervous breakdown, recounted how the last time the parasitic worms had invaded the book-filled study, they had eaten straight through *The Collected Works of Parnabus McCallister's Divining Spells*, all twelve volumes. But she snapped out of it in time to start pecking at the bookworms, while Gilbert lit some warding candles, which gave off plumes of smoke forcing their retreat.

The afternoon had been filled with wizarding chores as well: cauldron cleaning, wand polishing and dusting the hourglasses. They spent some time collecting mud lizards for regeneration potions — potions that Aldwyn was told would allow a missing arm or finger to grow back within minutes. It turned out Aldwyn had a particular knack for chasing these dirt-dwelling creatures made of living mud. He'd become quite comfortable digging through muck while living briefly in the sewers beneath Bridgetower, until the notorious crocodile infestation two years ago had made it too dangerous. He even got a compliment from Skylar for nabbing three mud lizards at once.

Before the sun had set, Aldwyn watched the young wizards-in-training create water fairies out of thin air and cast a spell that allowed a barren everwillow tree to grow back its leaves. And right before dinner,

Gilbert said this hadn't even been a busy day.

Aldwyn licked his bowl clean as embers popped and crackled right over his head. Dalton added some more kindling to the fire.

"The evening breeze is strong for early autumn," he said. "If the strange weather occurrences of late keep up, my father's barley crop will be a small one again. And I imagine Marianne and Jack's uncle will fare no better."

"Well, word has spread that Queen Loranella is ill," said Kalstaff. "Which would explain why her weather-binding spells have been unable to hold back the hail and mountain winds. And why there have been reports of gundabeasts breaking through her majesty's enchanted fences and roaming Vastia."

Marianne glanced up from her stew.

"I thought I saw something creeping outside our bedroom window last night," she said with a devilish grin.

"Stop teasing," said Jack, clearly alarmed.

"And it looked hungry."

"Now, now, Marianne," said Kalstaff. The old wizard waited until her giggling subsided, before continuing.

"Border monsters like the gundabeasts are very serious business. The longer the queen is in a weakened state, the greater these threats to Vastia will become."

"But you could defeat them, couldn't you, Kalstaff," said Jack, more as a statement of fact than a question.

"Nothing to be concerned about, Jack," said Kalstaff. "Not yet at least."

Aldwyn had never realised how important the queen's magic was in keeping Vastia safe.

"May we be excused?" asked Dalton. "I have some component charts to memorise before bed."

"Not just yet," said Kalstaff, as he turned to his youngest pupil. "First, it is time for Jack's Familiar Rite."

Jack jumped up excitedly, hurrying over to Aldwyn. He picked him up and brought him before Kalstaff, who was seated on a mossy rock.

"Sit him beside you and take his paw in your hand," instructed Kalstaff.

Jack sat cross-legged on the ground, scooping up Aldwyn's furry paw in his palm. There it was again: the warm, comforting sensation of belonging. It was the very same thing Aldwyn had felt in the familiar store when Jack first tickled his chin. Kalstaff began to draw circles in the air with his rod. Aldwyn glanced over to Gilbert, utterly confused by what was happening.

"Uh, what's going on?" asked Aldwyn.

"Shhh," whispered Skylar. "You'll disturb Kalstaff's incantation."

Kalstaff continued with the ritual, throwing a spray of copper dust into the fire, turning the flames green.

"*Vocarum animale,*" intoned Kalstaff. "*Assendix scientento felininum!*"

In a flash, the fire jumped into the sky and then just as quickly got sucked back into the logs, disappearing as if it had never been there in the first place. Jack and Aldwyn looked around, waiting for more to happen.

"That's it?" asked Jack.

"Will somebody please tell me what's going on?" asked Aldwyn.

Jack's head shot round to Aldwyn.

"What did you just say?"

"I said will somebody please – hang on, are you talking to me?" answered Aldwyn.

"Holy dragon eggs!" exclaimed Jack. "I can

understand you. Say something else."

"Um, OK: I... like... fish!"

"Wow! It worked. Now I suppose you can tell me your name."

"I'm Aldwyn."

"Nice to meet you, Aldwyn. I'm Jack," he said, before turning to the others. "His name is Aldwyn! He just *told* me."

"That is amazing," teased Marianne. "What else did he confide in you? That he likes chasing balls of wool?"

"You forget how excited you were when Gilbert first spoke to you," Kalstaff admonished her. "You nearly fainted."

"It's true," recalled Dalton. "Kalstaff had to carry you over to the runlet and splash water on your face."

Marianne blushed, and Jack let out a laugh.

"Pretty cool, huh?" said Gilbert to Aldwyn. "Kalstaff waves his wand a couple of times and next thing you know, your loyal gains the ability to understand what you're saying."

"It's a lingual divination spell," explained Skylar. "It only works between you and your loyal. It allows human spellcasters like Dalton or Jack or Marianne to commune with their familiars, even though they can't speak animal tongue the way elder wizards, like Kalstaff, are able to."

"I understand it's some of Ebekenezer's best work," said Aldwyn, taking the small titbit of knowledge he had overheard in the familiar store and claiming it as his own.

Skylar nearly sprained her neck, so severe was her double take.

"Horteus Ebekenezer," clarified Aldwyn, "The great forest communer."

"I didn't realise your studies were so advanced," said Skylar.

"Well," replied Aldwyn. "I may not know so much about juniper berries, but I do know my communers."

Kalstaff got up from the lichen-covered rock he was sitting on.

"Jack, this is the beginning of a long journey that you and Aldwyn will be taking together," he said. "No wizard can accomplish true greatness without a devoted familiar at their side. I know I couldn't have if it hadn't been for Zabulon, may the Gods rest his spirit."

Jack nodded, then looked at his new feline companion. Aldwyn glanced back up, saw the pride in the young boy's eyes and, to his surprise, felt a little proud himself.

"All right, time for bed," said Kalstaff to his three apprentices. "We leave for our walkabout at sunrise."

Everyone helped rinse the pots and pans and douse the firepit. Jack, the last to finish his chores, scooped up Aldwyn and headed for the cottage. They went straight to Jack's bedroom, which the boy shared with his sister and Gilbert. After a quick survey, Aldwyn decided the room was a bit confined for his taste. There were two straw cots placed side by side, while a small trunk rested against the wall, stuffed with all of Jack and Marianne's clothes. On a nearby table, a pear-shaped globe was slowly spinning on a needle, showing the lands of Vastia and beyond.

Gilbert fell asleep on a pillow at the foot of Marianne's bed and within two minutes was snoring loud enough to wake a hibernating cave troll. Jack folded up a blanket on the floor for Aldwyn to sleep on, then, after saying good night, got into bed himself.

Hardly a moment had passed before Jack

whispered in the dark, "Aldwyn, are you awake?"

"Yeah."

"Can I ask you something? Do you ever get seasick?"

"You mean like on a boat?"

"A boat, or a sailing skiff, or on the back of a travelling whale."

"I don't know. I've never been on any of those things. Why?"

"I was just thinking, after my wizard training is complete, we'll be going on a lot of adventures together. And I'd hate for you to get all green in the face every time we take to the water."

"Shhhhhh!" said Marianne from her neighbouring cot.

"Sorry," replied Jack before continuing in a whisper. "My mum and dad were Beyonders, you know. When I was a baby, they were sent on a secret mission to retrieve stolen treasure taken by the queen's jewel-keeper and his wife, who had raided the Palace Vault that they'd sworn to protect. My parents were lost at sea, but I'm going to find them one day."

"You never knew them?" asked Aldwyn.

"No. Marianne did. Just a little, though."

"I didn't know my parents, either. At least you have your sister. I never had any family."

"Well, you do now," said Jack.

Jack's hand reached down and stroked Aldwyn's back. Aldwyn immediately cosied up to his touch. He never would have expected to feel such a strong kinship with a boy who'd been a total stranger a mere two sunrises ago.

"Good night, Aldwyn."

"Night, Jack."

Moments later, Jack's breathing became heavy. The boy had fallen into a peaceful slumber.

Aldwyn tried to get comfortable, but unlike the first night, when he'd been too exhausted to care where he slept, tonight he simply couldn't fall asleep with a roof over his head. He decided he needed a breath of fresh air and crept to the hallway. As he passed Dalton's neighbouring room, he could see through the crack in the door that the boy was still awake, studying a scroll by candlelight.

Entering the living room, he spotted a window

that had been left ajar and quickly made his way towards it, passing the hammocks strung up in front of the fireplace. The room was much darker now, since the lightning bugs had gone to sleep in their hive. Hopping up onto a large oak table, Aldwyn paused to look at a framed painting of what appeared to be Kalstaff in his younger years, accompanied by another man wearing a robe just like Kalstaff's and a beautiful, imperial-looking woman in a long white dress. He recognised her as a younger Queen Loranella – there was a statue of her in front of Bridgetower's courthouse that Aldwyn used to sleep beneath on hot summer afternoons. Each of them was joined by what had to be their familiars: Kalstaff's bloodhound, the wizard's turtle and the queen's grey rabbit. Aldwyn continued along the table, past an enchanted quill that was busily copying Kalstaff's lesson plans for the next day, before bounding out of the window.

He immediately looked for the fastest route to the roof and spotted an orange tree whose branches brushed up against the tiles atop the cottage. As Aldwyn walked swiftly across the yard, he noticed that one of the spell library's windows was open. He didn't think much of it until he saw Skylar exit with a small leather-bound book tucked under her wing. He ducked out of sight as Skylar pushed the window shut with her beak before flapping off into the woods. Aldwyn found her actions curious and decided to follow her.

He stepped quietly through the dense underbrush on the edge of the woods until he arrived at a clearing. Fallen leaves of orange and green carpeted the ground, and at the centre, Skylar was perched upon a tree stump, the borrowed – or was it stolen? – book open before her. Aldwyn hid in the darkness, peering through a narrow gap between two massive oaks. Skylar flipped the pages of the book with her wing, looking purposefully for a passage of interest. Then she seemed to have found it. Aldwyn watched with growing curiosity as she plucked the carcass of a large beetle from her shoulder satchel and placed it beside her on the stump. Her eyes sped across the page of the book and then her clawed foot dived back into the satchel, removing a clawful of silver powder. She sprinkled some onto the beetle's carcass and read aloud from the tome.

"*Mortis animatum!*"

Aldwyn felt a chill tickle his ear, almost as if the air was whispering to him. Then, on the tree stump, the beetle's legs began to twitch. Aldwyn was quite certain the beetle had been dead just moments ago, so how could it be moving now? Skylar looked like she expected something more to happen. When it didn't, she buried her beak back into the spell book, and as she read, a gust of wind blew some of the leaves up off the ground, exposing what lay beneath them: a scattering of elk bones, left behind by forest-dwelling wolves. The same breeze sent the excess powder from the stump sprinkling down onto the gnawed skeletal remains. Skylar, still searching the text, failed to notice the bones of the great elk starting to reassemble themselves behind her. Aldwyn watched aghast and fascinated as the jigsaw puzzle of hooves and antlers pieced itself together, one cracked bone at a time. *What kind of dark magic is Skylar dabbling in?* Finally, she looked up, just in time to see the skeletal elk reborn. She seemed terrified and at the same time thrilled by what she had accidentally brought to life. Then the creature charged. Skylar instantly took to the air, as the reborn elk galloped blindly forwards. It was only then that Aldwyn realised that the creature was heading straight towards him. He braced himself as the skeleton collided with the trunk of the tree behind which he was hiding. When it hit, its bones shattered; rib cage, vertebrae and antlers split apart once more, dropping back down to the ground in a lifeless heap. Skylar, rather unbothered by it all, returned to the book and her beetle, but Aldwyn had no intention of sticking around to see what spell she would cast next. He high-tailed it out of there before he was spotted, thankful to still have his limbs intact.

Aldwyn ran for the cottage without looking back and leaped up the orange tree he had spotted earlier, effortlessly climbing up the bark and across the branch to the safety of the rooftop. Heart still beating, he sat himself down next to the weather vane, took a deep breath and peered out over the Aridifian Plains. Far, far away in the distance, he thought he could make out the light at the top of Bridgetower's spired watchtower. As he stared, Aldwyn thought of what this night would have been like back home: sleeping with one eye open, his paw clutching the scraps of food he had scrounged that day, guarding against other alley strays who would attack him for even the smallest morsel of fish. It had been the only life he'd ever known, orphaned as a kitten, with no memories of his mother or father or what kind of alley cats they must have been. But here in Stone Runlet he would walk a very different path, one that was dangerous and unpredictable, but also filled with a sense of purpose, of something larger than himself.

Aldwyn's eyes began to close. Both of them. So here he would stay. He would learn to be Jack's familiar, magic skills or no magic skills. *Familiar.* How strange that word sounded in his head, when in fact there was nothing familiar about this world to him at all.

FIVE

Walkabout

"Aldwyn!" cried Jack. "Aldwyn, where are you?"

Aldwyn stretched his legs as far as he could, still half asleep on the rooftop of the cottage.

"Aldwyn!" called Jack again, his voice growing more concerned.

Aldwyn's eyes opened wide and he quickly got his bearings. Giant puffy clouds were racing across the sky, swallowing up the sun for a moment, but burning off just as quickly as they had come. The autumn scent of falling leaves floated in the air, an unaccustomed smell to a cat who had spent his life in the city. He peered over the shingles and saw Jack searching the yard frantically, barefoot and still dressed in his cotton nightshirt.

"I'm up here," said Aldwyn.

When Jack saw his familiar, his face flooded with relief.

"What are you doing up there?" he asked. "I thought you'd run away."

"Sorry. I'm just used to sleeping under the stars."

"Well, come on. We have to get ready for our walkabout."

Aldwyn scurried across the tree branch and back down to the ground, walking up alongside Jack and rubbing his fur against the boy's legs.

"I better get changed," said Jack, bending down to scratch Aldwyn's ear. The alley cat's tail curled happily. "You should head over to the runlet and drink some water. It's going to be a long day."

"I'm not that thirsty," replied Aldwyn, wanting to avoid another run-in with the swimming eyeballs.

Jack ran back into the cottage and almost collided

with Dalton and Skylar as they were stepping out into the sunshine.

"Be sure to check your boots before you put them on," Dalton warned Jack. "I saw your sister carrying a handful of marsh berries."

"Hey, why do you have to ruin all my fun?" Marianne asked Dalton as she and Gilbert came outside right behind him. She gave Dalton a playful push, the kind fourteen-year-old girls give fourteen-year-old boys they like.

It wasn't long before Kalstaff emerged from the cottage dressed in his wilderness cloak with his rod floating by his side. Jack followed behind, now wearing a tunic with leather laces up the front.

"Today we shall walk to the edge of the borderland," announced Kalstaff. "Remember to bring your botanical field guides and a quill. You will be taking notes." Jack sighed at this, disappointed.

"Oh, and I almost forgot," continued the elder wizard. "Have any of you seen Wyvern and Skull's *Tome of the Occult*? It seems to have gone missing from the spell library last night." Aldwyn immediately knew the culprit and stole a glance at Skylar. She nervously shifted from one foot to the other, but nobody else seemed to notice. "I don't want to discourage private study, of course," said Kalstaff, "but let me warn you: this is a very dangerous book about necromancy, one whose spells of the dead can be corrupting in inexperienced hands."

A tense silence followed. Despite Skylar's earlier skittishness, she remained stone-faced, and Aldwyn was in no position to out her. With none of his pupils coming forward, Kalstaff let the issue go unresolved for now

"Very well then. Let us be off." Kalstaff waved his hand over his rod and it immediately transformed into a large walking stick. Aldwyn watched as the old wizard headed for the trees, which seemed to open a path for him.

Even on the sunniest of days, glorious days like this one, the Forest Under the Trees was cloaked in emerald shade. No ray of light could penetrate the 200-foot high canopy of green that protected the woodland floor below.

As they were heading deep into the shadowy forest,

Kalstaff began a long-winded lecture on the vegetative rarities unique to this isolated region, from lavender fungus to dew algae. Aldwyn could barely keep his eyes open as Kalstaff's lesson turned to such snooze-worthy topics as "proper ivy handling techniques" and "the advantages of chopped versus diced pine needles". He was more interested in looking up at the day bats that were flying in circles overheard.

Gilbert, who was lagging behind, stopped mid-hop as he passed a puddle of morning dew that had collected in an over-sized fern leaf.

"Whoa, I think I'm seeing something," said Gilbert to the two other familiars. "A vision. It looks like some kind of wyrm dragon."

Sklyar peered over his shoulder, then said in her usual exasperated tone, "You mean the reflection of that caterpillar up in the tree?"

Gilbert looked up to spy a black, prickly caterpillar that was clinging to a twig. "Huh. Well, puddle viewing isn't an exact science."

"Puddle viewing?" asked Aldwyn curiously.

"Gilbert comes from the Daku Swamp Forest," explained Skylar, "where all the tree frogs are born with the power of divination, able to see visions of past, present and future in pools of water."

"Clever," said Aldwyn, as the trio resumed their walk, following behind Kalstaff and the young wizards. "What kind of tricks can *you* do?"

"Tricks are for circus monkeys," Skylar responded, a little bit insulted. "I'm an illusionist, like all the birds from Nearhurst Aviary." Aldwyn wasn't entirely sure what sort of wizardry that entailed, but he was certain bringing the elk bones to life in the woods was well outside what she claimed her talent to be.

"Illusions are one of the most underrated circles of magic," continued Sklyar. "I can make things appear that are not really there. And oft times the appearance of something can be more powerful than the thing itself."

"It's kinda lame, if you ask me," chimed in Gilbert.

"Said the frog who thought he saw the future in the bottom of a pickle barrel," Skylar snapped.

"I had a premonition of being attacked by little hippopotamuses!"

"I think we've all agreed those were a handful of floating gherkins," said Skylar, rolling her eyes.

After a frustrated sigh, she turned back to Aldwyn. "I just hope what they say about you cats from Maidenmere is true. I mean, I assume that is where you're from. Maidenmere. Given your size and colouring."

"They say a lot of things about us Maidenmere cats," he replied, bluffing the best he could. "What exactly are you referring to?"

"You know, that your telekinetic powers can rival even those of the Gordian Mindcasters."

"Oh, I wouldn't go that far," he said. "But reading somebody else's mind is a nifty talent," he added, digging himself deeper still into a hole.

"Mind reading – that's telepathy," said Skylar. "Telekinesis is *moving* things with your mind."

"Right. That, too."

"You can do both?" Gilbert said excitedly. "Tell me what I'm thinking of right now."

"Uh… um…"

Skylar looked at Aldwyn sceptically. He swallowed hard, his paws moistening with sweat.

"A fly?" he guessed.

"No way! That's incredible," said Gilbert. Almost

against her will, Skylar seemed impressed too.

Aldwyn had, for the moment at least, escaped without having his true identity revealed – that he was not a familiar but a lowly alley cat. He was spared any further questioning by the group's arrival in a beautiful, moss-covered clearing, in the middle of which stood the biggest tree he had ever seen.

"Can anyone tell me what kind of tree this is?" asked Kalstaff, stopping.

"A colossus tree," answered Dalton.

"That's right."

Kalstaff used his thumbnail to puncture the soft bark of the tree. Crimson-coloured sap began to leak out of the hole.

"Who can tell me what this sap is used for?" asked Kalstaff. "Jack, do you want to make a guess?"

Jack nervously hummed and hawed, unsure of the answer.

Skylar leaned over to Aldywn and Gilbert and whispered, "When mixed with lava spice, it creates a serum that, even if you swallow only a single drop, can cause you to grow up to double your size."

Kalstaff looked to his other students. "Marianne, Dalton?"

They too were stumped.

"Well, then you'll have to look it up," said Kalstaff. "I'll give you a hint: it has to do with enlargement."

"You are such a show-off," said Gilbert to Skylar, annoyed and impressed in equal measure.

"Dalton, collect a sample for further study," instructed Kalstaff. The young wizard pulled a vial from his bag and began filling it with the colossus sap.

Gilbert poked his green elbow into Aldwyn's fur: "Hey, Aldwyn, what am I thinking about *now*?" he asked.

"Um, another fly?"

"That is insane! Get out of my head."

Kalstaff declared it was time for a short break and Jack wandered off to explore the clearing, with Aldwyn tagging along behind him. Between two rocks, glistening in the sun, Aldwyn spotted an elaborate web and in it a nimble creature with pearly white skin and wings that appeared too delicate to touch. "What's this?" Aldwyn whispered to Jack, afraid to disturb the creature. "It's a spider nymph," Jack whispered back excitedly. "They're incredibly rare." The two stood gazing at the winged arachnid, which proceeded to weave hypnotic patterns into its silk net. Soon the colourful web was drawing Jack and Aldwyn into some kind of trance.

"Don't stare too long," Marianne shouted from across the clearing. "Otherwise you won't be able to snap out of it."

Jack quickly blinked and turned away, but Aldwyn remained transfixed, the dizzying rainbow patterns reflecting in his eyes. The spider nymph began to move towards him, having successfully dazed its prey. Then, suddenly, the seemingly innocuous arachnid revealed a mouthful of venom-dripping fangs. Before the eight-legged predator could strike, Jack gave a tug on Aldwyn's fur and pulled him away. Disappointed, the spider returned to its web.

"Kalstaff has a saying," said Jack. "Oft times, the friendliest looking creatures are the ones that are most dangerous."

"*Now* you tell me?" asked Aldwyn.

The two shared a chuckle.

"Gather round," instructed Kalstaff, who was standing by the low-hanging limb of an Aridifian birch. The group formed a semicircle in front of him, each of the young wizards-in-training accompanied by their familiar. "Does anyone know what's special about this tree?"

Dalton immediately raised his hand.

"Yes, Dalton."

"The branches are wrapped in constrictor vines. The birch gives the vines food, while the vines protect the tree from birds and animals who might feed off its bark."

Skylar nodded in agreement from his shoulder.

"How do the vines protect the tree?" asked Jack.

Kalstaff answered by tapping one of the dangling vines with his walking stick. In the blink of an eye, the green vine wrapped around the stick and yanked it straight out of Kalstaff's hand. Gilbert leaped behind Marianne, a croak of panic escaping his lips.

"Marianne, I could use a little help here," said Kalstaff. "Use one of those withering spells you learned last week."

Marianne reached down and picked up a handful

of soil. She threw it into the air and called out, "From green to brown, drop that staff back on the ground!"

The vine shrivelled up, releasing the walking staff back into Kalstaff's waiting hand. Jack and Aldwyn exchanged an impressed look.

"Very good," said Kalstaff. "Nice technique."

Marianne shrugged off the praise, doing her best to hide how much Kalstaff's approval meant to her.

"All right, students, time to collect some clover," called Kalstaff, clapping his hands together. "I see a patch over there by the rocks. Even spells can use a dash of good luck mixed in."

Jack scooped up Aldwyn and ran to where Kalstaff had indicated. "I bet you I'll gather the most!" he shouted to Marianne and Dalton.

As Jack sprinted for the inch-high patch of shamrocks, Aldwyn was jostled back and forth in Jack's arms, feeling as if the fish and potato stew he'd had for dinner the night before might bounce right out of his stomach. But before Aldwyn could develop full-blown nausea, Jack set him down and started grabbing fistfuls of clover, shoving them into his pouch. Marianne and Dalton strolled up behind them.

"You're only supposed to take the ones with four leaves. Anything less can curse a whole spell," Dalton informed Jack impatiently. "And trust me. It's no fun having to sort through them later."

But Jack continued to pick every clover within reach, then suddenly stopped, curious, and called over to his familiar, "Hey, Aldwyn, look at this!"

Aldwyn, who still felt a little dazed from his close encounter with the spider nymph, reluctantly headed over towards Jack, who was pointing at what appeared to be a freshly dug hole in the ground. "It must be a mouse hole," Jack said.

Aldwyn tried to peer inside the hole. He could only make out darkness below, but felt a warm breeze. "It smells kind of sour," he said. Aldwyn's instincts were telling him that there was something very wrong with this hole.

"We found something over here," Jack called back to the others. "I think it's the burrow of a garden mouse."

"Mice don't dig in clover patches," replied Dalton.

"And it's kind of *big* for a mouse hole," mumbled Aldwyn, more to himself, as Kalstaff quickened his pace, coming up behind Jack and his familiar. A blast of hot wind blew through Kalstaff's moustache as he bent over to look at the hole.

"That's not a burrow. It's a breathing hole," he said with urgency. "Back away! Quick!"

But before any of them could take even one step, the earth exploded, sending Kalstaff, loyals and familiars flying backwards. Soil and rock debris rained down on them as a ten-foot-tall creature emerged from the ground with a deafening roar. It had three eyes, tough, plated, grey skin, thick hoofed feet and a horn jutting out of its forehead. Standing upright, the beast swung one of its clawed hands at Kalstaff, who blocked it with his staff.

"Gundabeast!" cried Gilbert.

"Familiars, take cover!" the old wizard shouted. "Jack, stay behind me. Marianne, Dalton, I'm going to need your help."

Skylar and Gilbert immediately took shelter behind the nearby rocks. Aldwyn was still shaking off the impact from the rain of rubble.

"Aldwyn, get over here!" yelled Skylar from across the clearing.

Aldwyn looked up and quickly dodged the gundabeast's giant fist. It hit the ground where Aldwyn had just been, leaving a crater among the clover. Aldwyn scrambled to get away as the three-eyed subterranean monster thrust its horned head downwards, preparing to stab him.

Nothing stood between Aldwyn and the creature's sharp ivory horn, until Jack, brave and more than a little reckless, dived on top of Aldwyn, shielding his familiar from the attack with just his body.

"*Gustavius rescutium!*" shouted Dalton from afar.

A moment before the horn tore into Jack's flesh, a small tornado of wind lifted both him and Aldwyn out of harm's way. The beast's horn came down hard, getting stuck in the ground. Dalton's spell dropped the boy and his familiar, breathless and a little shell-shocked, right beside Gilbert and Skylar.

Aldwyn looked up at Jack with awe and respect. No one had ever risked their life for his before. This was why animals called their human companions *loyals*.

"You could have been killed," said Aldwyn, overwhelmed with gratitude.

"I know you'd do the same for me," said Jack, as he rose to his feet and ran back towards Kalstaff.

"Jack, a shield spell would have been a lot safer," Aldwyn could hear Kalstaff scolding Jack, but not without a note of pride at the boy's bravery in his voice. "Next time, think before you act!"

"Exciting, isn't it?" chirped Skylar, high on the thrill of magical combat.

"If by exciting you mean terrifying, then yes!" said Gilbert.

Aldwyn watched as the creature pulled its horn out from the dirt. Now spitting mad, its three eyes fixed on Kalstaff and his young apprentices. The beast dropped onto all fours, kicking up dirt like an angry bull and roaring with rage.

"Now, who can tell me what a gundabeast's weak spot is?" Kalstaff shouted at his students over the noise.

"The neck!" called Jack from behind Kalstaff.

"Exactly."

The gundabeast began to charge forwards, heading straight at Kalstaff and Jack. Aldwyn watched as the earth splintered behind the creature.

Marianne sent a shower of sparks flying from her

hands. "Starburst, send your worst!" she incanted in a firm voice.

The sparks solidified into a bright beam of light that shot into the chink in the gundabeast's plated hide, right between its chin and its chest, stopping it in its tracks and causing it to let out a high-pitched squeak.

"Be gentle," said Kalstaff. "It's just a baby."

The beast swung its arms aimlessly, severing one of the forest's trees in half with its forearm.

"A very strong baby," said Gilbert, as he ducked further behind his cover.

Skylar spotted Dalton's pouch lying on the ground nearby. "Dalton, your pouch," she called to him. "Should I bring it to you?"

"Stay back, Skylar," he shouted. "It's too dangerous for you."

The blue jay hopped from her perch, considering whether to retrieve it anyway. Then she thought better of it, returning to her safe haven behind the rocks with Gilbert and Aldwyn, a little disappointed.

"Let's all join together to do a force push," said Kalstaff.

The three young spellcasters lined up in a row

beside him and they all put out the palms of their hands opposite the beast.

"Jack, find your focal point," advised Kalstaff. The boy's eyes narrowed. "Good!"

A large, ghostly hand formed between them and the lumbering creature from beyond the borderland, pushing the gundabeast backwards. Aldwyn watched, amazed at the display of magic before him. His respect grew stronger still for the power of these protectors of the queendom.

The hand continued to force the beast backwards, right up against the bark of the Aridifian birch tree. Upon contact, the constrictor vines coiled themselves tightly around the gundabeast's arms, capturing it. The gundabeast let out a roar of frustration as it struggled but failed to free itself from the green tendrils. Eventually, its roar subsided and gave way to pitiful squeaks.

"Well done. The constrictor vines should hold it for a few days. I'll contact the Council and have them send some beast tamers to escort it back to the Beyond," said Kalstaff, brushing some dried earth off his robe. "Now just because we've had a little excitement doesn't mean you're getting out of that pollen identification quiz I promised. Get out your field guides and quills."

The three young wizards groaned in protest and then sat down in the clover, preparing for a far less thrilling part of their walkabout. Aldwyn, Skylar and Gilbert came out from their hiding place. They tiptoed past the captured gundabeast, sneaking a closer look.

"You messed with the wrong bunch of wizards and familiars," said Gilbert cockily.

The gundabeast lunged forwards with a grunt and Gilbert leaped back in a panic, landing on his rear. Aldwyn and Skylar burst out laughing.

"What? I tripped," said Gilbert. Which made them laugh even harder.

By the time the group returned to Stone Runlet, night had fallen, and with the moon yet to rise even the dimmest stars were visible. Swirls of flickering lights coloured the sky, as if the star gods themselves had painted the heavens with fireflies. Kalstaff led his students and their familiars out from the woods and back towards the cottage.

The whole walk back home, Aldwyn had been lost in thought. If it hadn't been for Jack's bravery and Dalton's wind spell, the gundabeast would have flattened him into a cat pancake. Aldwyn was starting to realise that being a familiar came with its fair share of occupational hazards, but fortunately what seemed insurmountable for a cat or a blue jay or a frog could be handled with ease by the simple wave of a wizard's wand. He decided always to stick very close to Kalstaff and his three apprentices – especially Jack.

As the group passed the outdoor fire pit, Dalton turned to Jack. "Looks like we need some fresh wood for supper," he said. "Come give me a hand."

"I'll go and refill the canteens," said Marianne.

Just then, a bright light in the sky caught everyone's attention. Aldwyn looked up with the others and saw three shooting stars twisting around each other, ripping through the blackness above. The few clouds in the sky faded away, making sure everybody could see the trio of stars tango overhead. He didn't know why he knew, but Aldwyn was sure that what they were witnessing was an omen.

"Shooting stars!" said Jack. "Three of them."

The wizards and their familiars watched as the shooting stars fell somewhere just beyond Stone Runlet. Out of the corner of his eye, Aldwyn saw that Kalstaff, for a moment, appeared very upset, his whole demeanour changing. Seeing a look of such grave concern on the powerful wizard's face sent a shiver down Aldwyn's spine, all the way to the tip of his tail. But before anyone else caught a glimpse of the old spellcaster's worry, Kalstaff was smiling again.

"Come along, everyone," he said calmly. "We'll eat indoors tonight."

As Kalstaff quickly brought his three young students inside, only Aldwyn saw the wizard glance back and look anxiously at the horizon one last time.

SIX

Midnight Visitors

In the middle of the night, Aldwyn was woken by the heavy wooden door to the bedroom swinging open with a bang. He lifted his head from where it had been nestled next to Jack's side. His instincts told him there was danger in the air, and indeed a moment later Kalstaff was moving towards them with an intense but measured urgency.

"Children, wake up," commanded the old wizard. "We must go at once."

Marianne stirred immediately.

"What's going on?" she asked, scooping up a still-sleeping Gilbert from the pillow at the foot of her bed and retrieving her pocket scrolls from the wooden nightstand.

Kalstaff's knotty fingers reached out and shook Jack's shoulder.

"Now, Jack," he said firmly.

Jack's legs slid over and came to rest on the floor. He was still half asleep, not yet fully aware of the tenseness of the situation. Aldwyn sprang to his feet, his ears focused on a low rumbling in the distance.

"I can hear hooves in the sky," said Kalstaff. "I fear that danger is coming sooner than I expected."

Dalton appeared in the doorway with Skylar on his shoulder. She looked alert and ready for whatever was to come, carrying her leather satchel over her wing.

"Where are we going?" asked Dalton. "How many days' supplies will we need?"

"We're just heading across the glen to the cellar," said Kalstaff. "Come on."

Kalstaff ushered the apprentice wizards from the

room, leaving them no time to change out of their nightshirts or even put on their slippers.

"I thought Kalstaff didn't like to disturb the natural sleep cycle," Aldwyn said to Skylar, frightened by the midnight escape.

"He doesn't." This did little to reassure him.

Aldwyn's heart was racing. The pounding in his chest had begun the moment he'd been wrenched from his peaceful slumber and now it had reached a flat-out sprint. He stayed close to Jack as the boy staggered out of the room and down the hall. Gilbert had buried himself in Marianne's shirt pocket, his bulging eyes just peeking out over the edge.

In the living room, the wizards made some hasty emergency preparations before their exit. Kalstaff extended his hand and his rod flew off the table directly into his waiting palm. Marianne grabbed the lightning bug hive. Skylar glided from Dalton's shoulder down to a low-lying metal rack where she began filling her satchel with tiny glass vials containing different spell components.

Aldwyn could hear Gilbert muttering to himself from inside Marianne's pocket.

"Go to your happy place," he rambled in a mild panic. "A mosquito-filled swamp." But it didn't seem to help: Aldwyn could still hear the tree frog's rapid breathing.

Before leading his pupils from the cottage, Kalstaff stopped in front of the ancient weapons secured to the wall and unfastened the bronze clamps holding the spiked club, trident and halberd in place. Then he turned back to the door, leaving the sharpened blades on the wall.

"Aren't we taking them?" asked Jack.

Without reply, Kalstaff led the young wizards and their familiars outside.

A full moon was now hanging high in the sky, casting an eerie bluish light across the land. The tall grass swaying in the wind resembled stormy ocean waves. Kalstaff pointed across to the other side of the glen, where two closed iron doors marked the entryway to the cellar.

"Quick," said Kalstaff. "We'll be safe there."

They hurried across the cottage grounds, Marianne using the lightning bug hive to light their path. Stone Runlet, which had seemed so comforting and peaceful when Aldwyn had first arrived there, now was surrounded by the threat of an oncoming menace.

"If what we're running from is so dangerous, how will two metal doors protect us from it?" asked Marianne.

"There's more to that old earthen chamber than dilled apples and jugs of persimmon wine," said Kalstaff. "My father built it during the days of the Black March, back when I was a boy. He coated the inside with alabaster and sealed the walls with warding spells. These magic defences protected my parents and sisters when I was off fighting against the Dead Army Hordes. It will do the same for us."

He urged them on, but they hadn't even got halfway across the glen when a steady gallop of thunderclaps could be heard in the sky off to the northeast. Aldwyn looked up to see four spectral creatures coming towards them over the trees; horses that seemed to be formed out of translucent green energy. Through the sky they charged, cantering along a ghostly stone path that materialised before them and disappeared again once the last hoof was lifted from it. Atop the phantom stallions sat four riders, their identities hidden by the sinister darkness.

"Run!" said Kalstaff.

Jack, Marianne and Dalton didn't have to be asked twice. Aldwyn, terrified by the presence of evil in the atmosphere, bounded alongside them as their bare feet kicked up clouds of dust from the ground. Gilbert ducked even further out of view, as if the linen fabric of Marianne's shirt would keep him out of harm's reach. But the cellar doors were too far away; Aldwyn realised that they would never make it there in time.

And indeed, seconds later, the first horse, ridden by a slender figure wearing a charcoal robe, touched the ground. The other three landed right behind – soldiers outfitted in helmets, shining vests of chain mail and spiked armbands, with wicked looking swords at their sides. Kalstaff stepped forwards and held his arm out protectively, keeping himself between the unwanted visitors and his young pupils.

Green sparks ran up the legs of the spectral steeds and crackled down their manes and tails. The creatures smelled like a mixture of wet fur and the sky after a lightning storm. As the riders dismounted, the steeds seemed to fold in on themselves, becoming smaller and smaller until they were tiny balls of electrical energy, which vanished into thin air with a "pop".

The leader of the group stepped forward, folding the hood back from her head. Beneath it was revealed a distinguished-looking older woman, vibrant and strong for one as aged as she. She wore a band of platinum and gold around her head, gemmed rings of shimmering colours on her fingers and an ornately carved wooden bracelet around her wrist. Aldwyn could have sworn he'd seen her somewhere before. But where?

Kalstaff lowered his arm.

"Loranella," he said with a note of relief in his voice.

Of course! Aldwyn now recognised the woman as the queen. She had grown older since her face had been sculpted into the marble pedestal standing before Bridgetower's House of Trials, but her regal poise was still unmistakable.

"What brings you here at such an hour, my old dear friend? I thought you were ill," continued Kalstaff.

"Rumours of my sickness have been greatly overstated," replied the queen.

"I wish you had shot me a messenger arrow before

your arrival. You gave us all quite a scare."

"That was certainly not my intention. I apologise."

Kalstaff's shoulders relaxed, and the tension and worry that had gripped the wizards and familiars only moments ago was replaced by awe and respect for Vastia's great ruler, who was standing just a few feet from them. Gilbert decided to emerge from his hiding place and hop all the way down to the ground; Skylar meanwhile was rocking back and forth with excitement on Dalton's shoulder.

"To what do we owe this unexpected visit?" asked Kalstaff with a smile. "And since when did you start riding spectral steeds again? We haven't done that since the Uprising."

"The royal carriage is so formal. It just didn't feel like me any more."

"Is it true what they say?" asked Jack, wide-eyed with wonder. "Did you really behead the dark mages, Wyvern and Skull, with only two swings of your sword?"

Queen Loranella knelt down and looked at Jack, nose to nose.

"No. I did it with just one."

Jack's eyes grew even wider.

The queen stood tall again and her gaze moved from Jack to Marianne and then to Dalton.

"So you are Kalstaff's three pupils," said the queen. "Word in Vastia's wizarding circles is that great things lie in your futures." Aldwyn could see Dalton straighten himself with pride, an expression mirrored by Skylar, who perched proudly on his shoulder. "Which is why I'm here," she concluded, gently pushing the hair out of Jack's eyes with a smile. There was something very wrong with that smile, Aldwyn thought. Then Loranella spoke again and all of his worst fears came true: "Guards," the queen said coolly, "Kill them."

Aldwyn didn't want to believe his ears, and from the look on Kalstaff's face, neither did the old wizard. But that didn't stop him from aiming the circular glass tip of his rod at his three apprentices. "*Shieldarum resisto!*" Kalstaff shouted, and suddenly three large but delicate bubbles, looking as if they had just been washed off a bar of soap, came spinning through the air.

But before they reached Jack, Marianne and

Dalton, the queen pointed one of her rings at them. She flicked her finger and the ring shot out a trio of ruby needles that popped each of the protective spells in mid-air.

"Tsk, tsk, tsk," Loranella said, wagging her finger from side to side, clearly amused by Kalstaff's feeble attempt. Then she turned to her soldiers. "What are you waiting for? The prophecy ends here."

The guards advanced on Jack, Marianne and Dalton, readying their blades. Seeing one of the soldiers' chipped battlesword glint in the moonlight snapped Marianne out of her paralysis. As the soldier prepared to strike, she chanted, "Lich's eye, dragon's belly, turn that sword into jelly!"

The weapon made contact with Jack's shoulder, splattering his white shirt with globs of red. The sight gave Aldwyn a severe shock, tightening his chest and making him go weak in the legs.

"I'm bleeding!" cried Jack.

"No, that's just strawberry," said Marianne, as the guard lifted up the hilt of his sword. The blade was gone, having been transformed into jelly. Aldwyn breathed a sigh of relief; Jack was OK, for now at least.

The other two soldiers wasted no time and charged forwards with their deadly blades held over their heads. The first one tossed aside what was left of his weapon and grabbed a double-sided battleaxe that was strapped to his back.

"Get to the cellar," Kalstaff shouted. He closed his eyes and beckoned forth from the cottage the spiked club, trident and halberd of yore. The weapons crashed through the window and flew into the fray, defending the young wizards against the attacking guards as if wielded by unseen hands.

The loyals and their familiars took off running again. Aldwyn glanced behind him to see the enchanted weapons, kept afloat only by Kalstaff's spell, fighting the queen's three soldiers. The trident ducked and dodged, trying to fork the belly of one of the guards. The long, sharp metal edge of the halberd was quick enough to slice a gash in one of the sword-wielding henchmen's shoulders. But Kalstaff's concentration was too divided: the spiked club met a devastating blow as the battleaxe splintered the blunt wooden instrument in half.

"Old age has weakened you," mocked Loranella,

her nose twitching with delight. "Funny, because I seem to just keep getting stronger."

She conjured a ball of fire in her hand and hurled it at Kalstaff. He held up his arm to redirect it.

"What has corrupted your mind? A curse? Disease? You can be healed. I'll help you."

"It's far too late for that," said the queen as her black eyes narrowed coldly, a shimmer of pink behind them. "I'm going to feed your corpse to the bone vultures."

She clapped her hands together, sending out a beam of energy. Kalstaff grasped his rod in both hands, shooting forth a beam of his own. The two bursts of light smashed against each other, deadlocking in the air, neither wizard able to gain an advantage.

Skylar and Aldwyn arrived at the iron cellar doors first. Jack, Marianne and Dalton got there moments later. Gilbert lagged behind, hopping as fast as his legs could carry him. Aldwyn realised they were just a swing of the door and a jump away from safety: below the ground, behind the alabaster-coated walls of the cellar, they would be protected. But just as Marianne reached for the latch, a pale orange stream of light shot over her shoulder, striking the metal cellar clasp and encasing it in a thick layer of rust. The loyals and familiars spun around to see that the bolt had come from Loranella, who while engaged in the stand-off with Kalstaff had been able to use a ring from her other hand to cast the spell. Marianne tried to pull the doors open anyway, but the queen's rusting bond held fast.

"Skylar, I need some ground glow-worm," said Dalton. "It's the only thing that can eat through the rust."

Skylar immediately dived with her beak into her leather satchel and began rummaging for the necessary vial.

"It's not here," she said with a look of utter confusion.

"What do you mean it's not there?" asked Dalton.

Before Skylar could answer, Jack spoke up sheepishly. "I borrowed it." All eyes turned to him. "I'm sorry. I was trying to make my marbles glow in the dark. But there's still some left over. It's in my pouch, on the nightstand."

They all looked back towards the cottage and the perils that lay between.

"It's too dangerous," said Marianne. "There's no way any of us could make it there and back unharmed."

"Aldwyn can do it," said Jack.

It took Aldwyn a moment to realise what Jack had suggested. "I can?" he asked out loud.

Just then, the queen used her free hand to shoot forth another ring blast, this one intended to burn the young wizards alive. Dalton conjured a swirl of wind to lift a fallen everwillow branch from the ground to intercept it. Upon contact, the branch exploded in a shower of flaming wood chips.

"Aldwyn, go!" pleaded Jack as he took cover from the raining embers.

Aldwyn thought he was much too young to die a heroic death, but what else was there to do? Besides, if there was one thing he was good at, it was running. And so the alley-cat-turned-familiar ran – right through the legs of the guard with the battleaxe, who was now fighting the two halves of the spiked club – just beneath the concentrated waves of energy radiating from Kalstaff's rod and Loranella's fingertips, as the two wizards remained locked in deadly battle – and straight for the front door of the cottage.

Miraculously, Aldwyn got there unharmed. Once inside, he darted down the hall to the bedrooms. He didn't stop until he arrived at Jack and Marianne's room. There, sitting beside the pear globe, was Jack's pouch. Aldwyn jumped atop the cot before leaping to the nightstand, where he snatched the leather bag in his teeth. Now all he had to do was go back the way he had come.

As he took a deep breath in preparation for another mad dash, he felt a hot tickle brush from his nostrils all the way into his throat. He realised that the room was beginning to fill with smoke and that the ceiling was on fire. One of Loranella's ring blasts must have set the cottage ablaze. Aldwyn high-tailed it for the hall, but before he reached the exit, one of the flame-licked ceiling beams collapsed, knocking the bedroom door clean off its hinges and toppling towards him. Aldwyn slid beneath it, narrowly avoiding the burning wall of wood.

With Jack's pouch secured in his mouth, he ran down the hallway and found the living room had become a crackling inferno, making the smithy's furnace seem cool by comparison. Roof shingles were dropping through the ceiling, shattering as they hit the ground below. The hammocks, once hanging peacefully, now looked like flaming spiderwebs, ready to grab Aldwyn in their tangle of burning rope. But he dodged the obstacles before bounding out through the doorway

He quickly saw that the situation outside had got significantly worse. Kalstaff had been forced to his knees and was struggling mightily to fight back the queen's relentless onslaught of magic. In his weakening state, Kalstaff's ability to control the floating weapons had diminished enough for the soldiers to gain the upper hand. Only the halberd remained fighting, with the club and trident fallen. Two of Loranella's soldiers were almost upon the young wizards, who still were trapped outside the rusted cellar doors. Aldwyn could see Skylar flying out from the woods, a small dark cloud following behind her. The brave blue jay flung a barrage of yellow storm berries at the approaching soldiers, causing a sheet of rain to fly in their faces. A small lightning bolt struck the helmet of the guard with the battleaxe, sending a current of highly charged particles coursing through his metal skull-cap. He tore it off his head to reveal a large patch of smoking scalp: half of his hair had been singed off. As Skylar took another flyby, he swung his helmet angrily, clipping her wing and sending her tumbling into the grass.

Aldwyn's charge across the glen was stopped short by the sound of shattering glass as the tip of Kalstaff's rod broke into a thousand pieces. It was followed by a haunting wail that seemed to come from the broken rod itself. Loranella wasted no time and struck the disarmed wizard with all of her evil-hearted sorcery. A spear of hot white energy seared a hole straight through Kalstaff's chest. As the wizard collapsed, the entire world seemed to freeze in horror and despair. For a moment, the eerie stillness of death hung over Stone Runlet.

Then Marianne screamed "No!" and time started moving again. The queen faced her soldiers. "Kill them. Kill them all," she screamed, motioning to the young wizards.

With her back now turned, she didn't notice Kalstaff stir from the dirt, his lips forming the all but inaudible words, "*Shieldarum resisto.*" The spell barely escaped his mouth, but again three shimmering bubbles formed in the air, only this time they didn't look nearly as delicate as they had before, glowing brighter and bolder as they spun rapidly towards his young apprentices.

"Talk about déjà vu," said the queen as she fired three more ruby needles from her ring at the bubbles floating by her. But now, when the red tips of her bolts hit the protective shells, they didn't puncture them; they merely bounced off. "What?" Loranella exclaimed, unable to hide her surprise and dismay.

Before she could make another attempt to destroy them, the three bubbles encircled Jack, Marianne and Dalton, melding to their bodies and creating a thin, impenetrable forcefield around each one of them.

The queen glared down at Kalstaff, who was pale and motionless and to Aldwyn seemed even more wrinkled than before.

"You used your last pulse of life for that? To cast three Astraloch bubbles? They won't protect them for long, Kalstaff." She shook her head dismissively and turned to her guards: "Bind them, tie them and take them away. We will kill them when the spell wears off."

Aldwyn dropped the pouch from his mouth. *What good would the glow-worms do now that the young wizards had been captured?*

Queen Loranella walked up to the captured wizards with a hop in her step. She whistled, and four balls of green energy appeared in the air, quickly unfolding into the four spectral steeds. Each of the three soldiers hoisted one of the bound children atop their horse before mounting it. Aldwyn could only watch helplessly as Jack's pleading eyes cried out for help. The queen pulled herself onto the last of the phantom stallions and, without looking back once, commanded: "Ride."

The ghostly path materialized again, curving away into the sky. On it, the steeds galloped away and were soon swallowed up by the darkness.

Silence descended quickly and without warning. It was as if the insects, brook and wind all dared not speak. Aldwyn stood in a daze. Gilbert hobbled over from where he had been kicked aside by one of the guards. Then the two spotted Skylar lying beak down in the dirt. They ran over to their comrade.

"Skylar," called Gilbert, nudging her with his foot. "Wake up!"

The jay flew up into the air with a start, wings beating and head spinning frantically. "Where are they? What happened?"

Aldwyn and Gilbert exchanged a look.

"What is it? Is Dalton OK? Tell me!" demanded Skylar.

"They've all been kidnapped," said Gilbert. "And the queen…"

Then Skylar looked over and saw Kalstaff lying on the ground. Like a dart, she flew to his side. Aldwyn and Gilbert quickly followed. Gathering before him, the familiars found Kalstaff breathing heavily, his cloak hiding the severity of his wound. The old wizard tried to clear his throat.

"Familiars, come close and listen carefully," he whispered weakly. "I am afraid a great responsibility has fallen on your shoulders. I wish it weren't so, but my path ends here." He coughed, then licked his lips before continuing. "Earlier this evening, I saw a prophecy, three stars spinning in the sky. It foretold that three young spellcasters from Stone

Runlet were destined to save this world: Marianne, Jack and Dalton. It is clear they have powers that are yet untapped, powers that could change the tide of what I fear may be coming. And it is now evident that I was not the only one who saw this prophecy."

"The queen," said Skylar, explaining to Aldwyn and Gilbert.

"Yes. The enchantment I bestowed upon your loyals will protect them for three sunsets. After that it will fade and they will be defenceless against the queen's deadly magic." Kalstaff's last breaths grew near. "You must find a way to rescue them. It is up to you."

"Us? How?" asked Aldwyn in disbelief.

"We're just a bunch of familiars," added Gilbert, shaking his head.

Even Skylar had a look of uncertainty on her face.

"I see the worry on your faces, but fear not. Heroism appears in many forms," said Kalstaff in a whisper. "Not always man or woman, but also fur, feather and tongue."

Kalstaff's eyes closed, never to open again. The once mighty wizard was dead.

Skylar flew gently atop him, nuzzling her feathered head into his chest. Gilbert stepped into his cold, open palm. Even though he had hardly known Kalstaff, Aldwyn, too, was overwhelmed by a feeling of profound loss. He had never experienced death before, at least not that of someone close to him. The only thing comparable was the feeling of heartbreak he endured from never having known his parents.

As the animals said their last goodbyes, a circle of mist formed a stone's throw away, and out from the fog, a faintly glowing bloodhound emerged, old and tender-looking.

Gilbert looked up at the canine spirit.

"Zabulon," he said.

Skylar lifted her beak, wiping away a tear with her wing. She too recognised the ghost of Kalstaff's familiar, his drooping ears and long face.

"Take good care of him," she said. "Guide him gently into the Tomorrowlife."

Zabulon approached Kalstaff, his steps light and buoyant, freed from the gravity that burdens all living beings. He leant his head down and took hold of the deceased wizard's hand before giving a pull. Aldwyn and the others watched as, gently, Zabulon tugged Kalstaff's spirit from his body. The transparent figure rose to his feet and turned to the mist without looking back. Together, the ghostly wizard and his familiar walked into the fog, reunited again.

Kalstaff was gone, the cottage had burned to the ground, and the young wizards were in the clutches of the evil queen. The three animals were on their own, an impossible task weighing heavily on their small shoulders. Aldwyn had but one question in his mind: *How had the fate of Vastia fallen upon a tree frog, a blue jay and himself, a fake familiar without even the tiniest whisker of magic?*

SEVEN

Into the Unknown

Four small grey clouds rained over what was left of the cottage as Skylar dropped storm berries into the flames. Sheets of water doused the blackened rooftop, sending steam drifting into the air. Aldwyn's heart ached upon seeing the now charred walls. He was hesitant to even look inside, not wanting to further tarnish the sweet memories of his all-too-short time here in Stone Runlet.

Nearby, a flock of shovel bills, with beaks like

curved spades, had descended to Kalstaff's side and were in the process of burying the great wizard's corpse under a pile of freshly dug earth. These peaceful birds travelled far and wide, only stopping when they sensed a spirit headed for the Tomorrowlife.

"I just don't understand," said Gilbert, pacing back and forth. "How are we supposed to rescue Marianne, Jack and Dalton? Our magical abilities are nothing compared to the queen's. We're familiars – assistants, helpers, the ones who get carried around in the wizard's pockets. We don't do the saving."

"True, this has never been asked of a familiar before," said Skylar. "I just don't see what choice we have. I might have suggested enlisting the help of Galleon, but according to his last letter to Kalstaff, he and Banshee are sailing the Ebs fighting off river dragons. Or perhaps we could turn to Sorceress Edna, but her manor in the Palace Hills is at least a two-day journey from here. And there's no guarantee she'd even be there, given her regular trips into the Borderlands. I'm afraid we're on our own."

Aldwyn certainly didn't like the sound of that. Although he never needed a human to protect him in

Bridgetower, out here it was different. He had seen first hand how dangerous these lands could be. Without the help of a wizard at their side, even a journey into the neighbouring forest could be deadly for a familiar, let alone another attack by the queen.

"We should collect what we can from the cottage before leaving Stone Runlet," continued Skylar. "We'll search high and low for our loyals, every corner of Vastia, until we find them."

"In three days?" asked Gilbert, already hopeless.

Skylar ignored him, flapping towards the burnt frame of the small house. Aldwyn and Gilbert walked behind her, entering through a singed gap in the wall. Inside, the once cosy dwelling was practically unrecognisable. It was difficult to believe Loranella's attack had destroyed so much so quickly.

"The components," lamented Skylar as she looked to the metal rack, where all that was left was melted glass and dust. "Wonders from lands distant and near – cobra scales and echo drool, dried rigour weed and amethyst powder – all lost to the fire." She seemed close to tears.

Aldwyn tried to feel sympathetic, but he couldn't really waste time crying over spell ingredients, rare though they might be.

"The library," said Skylar, as she flew through another gaping hole straight into Kalstaff's book-filled study, or what was left of it. "A trove of irreplaceable knowledge – no more!"

Then Aldwyn heard a groan so full of pain he thought Gilbert had injured himself.

"My fruit flies!" cried the tree frog.

Aldwyn watched as Gilbert raced frantically past the cooking pots and pans to the crispy black soot counter, where a broken clay pot was shattered with charcoal dust surrounding it.

"Gone. All of them gone!" moaned Gilbert, running his fingers through the charred remains.

"It'll be OK, Gilbert," Aldwyn said comfortingly. "We'll find more."

Gilbert desperately poked his tongue into the pot's pile of ash, but recoiled with a cough. "Not good, not good," he wheezed.

Skylar spotted some nightshade that had survived the blaze beneath one of the cooking pots and gathered it into her satchel. Gilbert bounced down from the counter and splashed into a puddle on the ground left from the storm berries. Aldwyn pawed through more of the wreckage in search of anything that might be useful on their journey.

"Guys!" Gilbert shouted. "Get over here. I'm having a puddle viewing."

Skylar looked back sceptically, doubting Gilbert's claim.

"No, really. It's Marianne, Jack and Dalton. I see them!"

Aldwyn and Skylar hurried over to Gilbert's side to catch a glimpse of the vision. And indeed, there in the pool was the rippling image of their loyals. They were chained to a wall, arms overhead, looking frightened but unharmed. Jack tugged futilely at his shackles, trying to wriggle free.

"You can do it, Jack," Aldwyn whispered. He extended a paw towards Jack's reflection, wishing to touch him, comfort him somehow.

"It's no use," they could hear Dalton's voice coming from the puddle. "I already told you, they're dispeller chains. They prevent us from casting magic."

Jack gave up the struggle and sank down to his knees.

"Don't cry, little brother," said Marianne. "As long as we are protected by Kalstaff's spell, she can't hurt us."

"It's not going to last forever," said Dalton, unable to keep the dread out of his voice.

Then the image began to swirl away,

"Find out where they are," Skylar urged Gilbert. "Quick!"

"It doesn't work like that," Gilbert snapped back. "It only shows you what it wants to show. Slivers of the picture, not the whole thing!"

"Just try," she said.

"Where is the queen hiding you? How do we save you?" Gilbert called out frantically to the wizards, even though they couldn't hear him. "Puddle, tell me!"

As the vision faded into nothingness, a soft murmur could be heard from the water, but the words were hard to understand. "What was that?" asked Gilbert, pressing his ear to the shallow pool. "Grey hair witch?" he repeated aloud, hoping for some kind of confirmation. But the water had gone silent.

"Don't look at me," said Skylar to Gilbert. "I don't speak puddle."

Aldwyn stared at the tree frog, waiting for something more.

"Grey hair witch. That's what the puddle said. I know it's not much help. I'm sorry."

But suddenly, Skylar didn't look disappointed at all. "Don't you see?" she said excitedly. "*Grey hair witch*. Agdaleen, the grey-haired witch! The queen must have a dark partnership with her – some kind of agreement that Agdaleen will keep them captive. She lives north of here, in the Weed Barrens."

"How do you know where she lives?" asked Gilbert.

"I read all about her in Wyvern and Sk…" She caught herself mid-sentence and quickly stopped. "It's common knowledge. Everyone knows Agdaleen's whereabouts."

Her slip up didn't go unnoticed by Aldwyn, but what Skylar was reading in her spare time was hardly important now.

"Well, now we know our destination," said Aldwyn. "But do either of you know how to get there?"

Skylar turned, glancing around the room. "Scribius!" she called out.

Skylar and Gilbert waited, while Aldwyn looked at them, puzzled. What was left in this empty shell of a house? Then, from the pile of ash where the table once stood, Kalstaff's enchanted quill, the one Aldwyn had seen writing out the old wizard's lesson plans, emerged. The magical writing tool, with its silver nib tarnished and feather tip scorched, limped towards them.

"Draw us a map to the Weed Barrens," Skylar instructed it.

Scribius shuffled across the floor to one of the few pieces of parchment that had survived the inferno. It began to sketch out a path on the page, inking in trees and valleys and roads en route to their destination. The pen was no expert cartographer, but its crude map would suit them just fine.

Skylar reviewed the course laid out before them. "This could take us over a day by foot. But if I flew ahead without you, I fear that it could be too dangerous, even for me." She looked up through the collapsed hole in the roof. Aldwyn followed her gaze and saw the sky's blackness fading to purple as the sun began to rise. "We have little time to waste."

Skylar rolled up the map with her claws and placed it in her satchel. Scribius, not wanting to be left behind, hurried into the satchel as well. Skylar took wing to the door, and Aldwyn and Gilbert followed. Once outside, the group walked across the glen, in the direction of the cellar. Aldwyn noticed Jack's pouch lying on the ground. He had forgotten about it since tossing it aside after the wizards' kidnapping. Thinking its contents might serve them well later, he slipped the strap over his head and tightened it with his teeth, so that the leather bag hugged his side. Skylar, who had already flown ahead to the edge of Stone Runlet, was peering north off into the distance. Gilbert and Aldwyn stepped up behind her and looked out at the rolling hills and forests through which their journey would take them.

"We'll have to travel at a horse's pace," said Skylar, before taking the lead down the hill.

Gilbert hopped after her, his head popping out above the tall blades of grass with each leap.

Aldwyn, however, hesitated and turned to the

southwest, where he knew Bridgetower lay, the high beacon of the city's watchtower shrouded in the morning haze. For a moment, he considered leaving all this madness behind and returning to the predictable perils of the walled city. He questioned his courage in the face of all the dangers sure to stand in his way should he continue forth with Skylar and Gilbert. It would be far easier to go back to his life as an alley cat of ill repute. But something kept his paws from running, feelings he had never experienced before. Obligation, loyalty to Jack, a call to something larger than himself; these noble emotions were now coursing through his veins, driving him towards something unexpected. And so he made his choice, taking a step to the north, into the unknown.

"I can see why humans wear shoes," said Gilbert, wincing. "A tree frog's feet are not made for this kind of travel."

Two hours had passed since the familiars had left Stone Runlet, and they were still traversing the wide expanse of the Aridifian Plains. The morning sun was climbing higher into the sky. Occasionally, it was covered by swiftly moving clouds that cast shadows across the land, creating an ever-shifting checkerboard of light and dark patches. There was little of note on the trail, save for a stalk covered in corn beetles; shiny yellow insects that could shave an ear of corn down to its cob in a blink. Gilbert's tongue had snared the lot of them, enjoying their salty, buttery taste.

The familiars came up over the next rise and spotted a well-trodden dirt road twisting away into the distance. As they began their descent, Aldwyn kept his eyes on the ground before him, wary of the sharp thistles sticking out from the pebbly earth.

"Ow, ow, ow," said Gilbert each time his slimy skin brushed up against the prickly vegetation.

With his head still cast downwards, Aldwyn noticed the shadow of a cloud that was now beneath his feet. It strangely resembled a large bird. He would have shrugged it off – after all, it was possible to see all kinds of creatures in the clouds – had he not heard something that sounded like a hundred boulders rolling down a mountain. The ground and the sky shook. Aldwyn looked up and saw six hawks beating their wings overhead.

"Tremor hawks," said Skylar, in a way that made it clear to Aldwyn that this was not good news.

Aldwyn watched as they circled above, leaving splintery cracks in the air. The avian predators had their eyes fixed on them and their sky-shaking vibrations were coursing through Aldwyn's body.

"We need to run for cover," cried Gilbert.

"Where?" asked Aldwyn, searching the treeless hill.

"Just stay close to me," said Skylar as she soared down to the ground between them. She closed her eyes and began waving her wings in the air, chanting to herself: "*Illusionaurum kiayn!*"

The tremor hawks dived straight for them, beaks open and talons outstretched, and Aldwyn wondered if their journey had come to an end before it had even properly started. Then a thick log materialised around the three familiars. Aldwyn was curious what kind of tricks his eyes were playing on him, but clearly their attackers saw it too, coming to an abrupt midair halt as they were faced with what appeared to be solid wood.

"Why are they stopping?" asked Aldwyn quietly.

"It's an illusion," said Gilbert. "We can see out, but all the hawks see is a fallen log."

"And I can't hold it much longer," said Skylar, her wings trembling.

The hawks continued to hover just yards above them. The skyquakes their wings were generating made Aldwyn's teeth chatter. Then, just as suddenly as they had arrived, they jetted back into the sky, off to search for new prey.

Skylar lowered her wings and the illusion faded.

"That was close," she said. "Tremor hawks are not an enemy a familiar would want to face without a wizard present. They've been known to topple castles when agitated."

The three animals resumed their walk down the gravelly path. Aldwyn remembered Skylar saying that the appearance of an object could be as useful as the thing itself, and he was beginning to understand what she had meant by that. The illusion of the log had saved them from being eaten. He was also quickly learning that in the world of magic, even someone as small as Skylar could wield great power.

"Hey, Aldwyn, take a whiff of this," called Gilbert,

who had hopped over to a patch of brown grass.

Aldwyn walked over to the tree frog, but he didn't have to get very close before his nose recoiled from a horrible odour.

"Ew, what is that?" asked Aldwyn, cringing.

"Stinkweed," said Gilbert with a smile. "Brings back memories. One time, Marianne put a clump of the grass in Dalton's pillow. His hair smelled like rotten lizard eggs for a whole week."

Aldwyn had a good chuckle. Even Skylar smiled at the recollection.

"Marianne's always loved a good practical joke," continued Gilbert. Then he sighed. "She's going to be OK, isn't she?"

"Don't worry. We'll find them," said Skylar reassuringly. "We'll do whatever it takes."

Aldwyn was struck by Skylar and Gilbert's devotion to their loyals, but he understood it well: in just a few days, he had already forged an inseparable bond with Jack. He could only imagine the kind of dedication years of companionship might bring.

"Now come on, the main road is down below," Skylar added, quickly returning to the task at hand.

"We should be able to follow it all the way to the Weed Barrens. If all goes according to my plan, our loyals should be safe before nightfall."

"What plan?" asked Gilbert.

"Once we find Agdaleen's lair, I'll distract the grey-haired witch with an illusion," said Skylar. "Then Aldwyn can use his telekinesis to unlock the dispeller chains. After that, Dalton, Marianne and Jack can do the rest."

Aldwyn got a sick feeling in his stomach, one that was even worse than the time he lapped up spoiled milk by the Glyphstone in Bridgetower. His telekinesis was part of the plan? He didn't have telekinesis. He had to tell them the truth, even though his new companions would surely want nothing to do with him once he did.

"Skylar," Aldwyn said quietly. "There's something I need—"

Suddenly, Gilbert's head perked up and he said, "Do you hear that?"

Skylar's attention quickly turned away from Aldwyn. His confession would have to wait. As the rumbling noise grew nearer, Aldwyn braced himself for a return of the tremor hawks or another gundabeast attack. Then he relaxed upon recognising the familiar sound: wagon wheels. Further down the hill he spotted a farmer steering a horse-drawn cart carrying bales of straw.

"Let's hitch a ride," said Aldwyn.

"And how do you expect us to do that?" asked Skylar. "You think that farmer is just going to let us take a free ride?"

"I wasn't planning to ask permission," said Aldwyn. "We can jump on the back."

"While it's moving?" croaked Gilbert

Skylar considered the idea. "It would save us hours. We could reach the Weed Barrens before high sun."

"There's no way we can catch up with it now," said Gilbert, as the wagon headed downhill for the woods, gaining momentum and distance.

"I've caught up with carriages going a lot faster than that," said Aldwyn. Skylar gave him a curious look. "When they happened to pass through Maidenmere, that is."

The trio hurried to the base of the hill. Skylar effortlessly flew to the cart. Aldwyn bounded: front paws, then rear paws, front, then rear. This was a skill he had perfected after years of daily practice. He made a running jump and his nails dug into the wooden planks on the back of the wagon. He hoisted himself up and turned back to see Gilbert struggling to keep pace.

"Come on, Gilbert," he called out.

"We can't miss this opportunity," cried Skylar, as if the tree frog needed the added pressure.

Gilbert's back legs pushed off the ground and he flew through the air. Aldwyn reached out a paw to grab him, but his hop didn't have the height or the distance. Gilbert landed with a thud on the ground, and the wagon continued to roll, the horses now moving at a fast trot. The tree frog picked himself back up and started hopping again. He huffed and puffed, and his slender orange feet moved faster than they'd ever moved before. He leaped again, and this time Aldwyn poked his claws into a stalk of straw on the cart and stretched it out as a lifeline. Gilbert grabbed hold of the fragile branch, but before Aldwyn and Skylar could pull him aboard, the stalk snapped and Gilbert went tumbling back towards the ground. But this time, the tree frog thought fast, shooting out his tongue and wrapping it around Aldwyn's paw. Aldwyn gave a tug and Gilbert flew into the back of the wagon, toppling Aldwyn onto the straw-covered wood planks.

"I did it," said Gilbert breathlessly. He collapsed onto his back, gasping for air. "I did it."

Then, without warning, the horses came to a sudden stop.

"Grazing time," called out the farmer, pulling his mares to the side of the road, where they began to feed on the grass.

Gilbert gave an exasperated sigh and wheezed: "I... just did all of that... for nothing?"

Aldwyn and Skylar couldn't stop themselves from bursting into laughter.

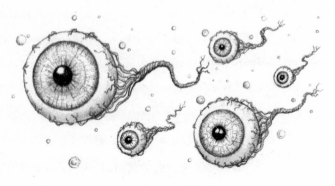

EIGHT

Agdaleen and the Octopot

Aldwyn's nose lifted into the air, sniffing excitedly. For the last three hours, he had been lying on a bed of he had made for himself, lulled into a pleasant sleep by the gentle swaying of the wagon and the *clop-clop-clopping* of horseshoes. Now his nostrils flared as he breathed in his favorite smell: fresh fish! When he lifted his head up over the wagon's side rail, he saw Split River, a sprawling port town divided in half by the wide blue river Ebs. A dense mist hung in the air, as if the clouds themselves had lazily nestled on the rooftops for a mid-afternoon nap.

"This is where we get off," said Skylar, as the cart reached a fork in the road and began heading east. "We'll have to walk the rest of the way to the Weed Barrens."

Aldwyn gave Gilbert a nudge, stirring him from the snooze he was taking in the shade of a water jug.

"Wake up," said Aldwyn, but Gilbert didn't budge. Aldwyn tried a different method. "Gilbert, look, fruit flies!"

Gilbert immediately snapped awake. "What? Where?"

"Oh, too late, you missed them," said Aldwyn, winking to Skylar. Gilbert was too befuddled to realise he had been duped. He barely had time to stretch before Aldwyn took a leap off the back of the wagon. His feet touched down on the muddy ground and he used his feline nimbleness to land smoothly. Gilbert jumped next, tumbling as he hit the ground. Aldwyn watched as the wagon, which had shortened what would have been a full day's journey into a brief trip, disappeared down the road.

"We go north and follow the river from here," said Skylar as she flew over to their sides. "We aren't far now."

Aldwyn still hadn't told Skylar and Gilbert about his lack of a magical talent. He didn't want to risk getting sent home. Not before seeing Jack one more time.

The three animals walked a path along the cliffs beside the Ebs. Not long into their trek, they passed a metal plate embedded in the side of a large rock. A blue gem sparkled in its center.

"This is where The Turn took place," said Skylar, stopping to point her wing first to the monument, then to the river. "See how the Ebs takes that sharp bend?" Aldwyn followed the trail of her feather to where the waters bashed up against the cliffs before heading southward. "That was the work of a spell cast long ago. A great wizard stood here. His name has been lost to time, but he was a man like no other. On the fiftieth day of the Unstoppable Storm, when the river was close to rising beyond its banks, he lifted those cliffs out from the earth to prevent all the lowlands from flooding. He literally turned the course of the Ebs forever."

Aldwyn could sense how greatly she admired Vastia's human elders.

"And it was men and women like him – wizards who forged these lands and made Vastia the great queendom that it is today – who were generous enough to pass magic down to the animals."

As they continued their hurried pace north, Aldwyn asked Gilbert, "Do you know all of this stuff, too?"

"Oh, no. History was never really my strong suit," he answered. "Of course, neither was arithmetics. Or astronomy. Or geography for that matter. Although I do have a knack for writing love poems. Care to hear one?"

"Maybe some other time," said Aldwyn politely.

"Lily pad, flat and round, my heart doth beat, oh what a sound," Gilbert recited from memory, ignoring Aldwyn's answer.

Their travels led them higher. The sandy banks of the Ebs soon turned to rock and gravel. Aldwyn was treated to some more of Gilbert's original sonnets, and the tree frog even threw in a handful of haikus to show his range. Skylar never slowed, but that didn't stop her from pointing out other historical markers of interest. It was just before high sun, as she was describing the ancient Warlock Trail – a racepath around Vastia where once a year noblemen and women competed in a triathlon of foot racing, wand flight, and spectral steeding – when Aldwyn noticed something very unusual following them. They resembled the swimming eyeballs from Stone Runlet, only instead of tails, these egg-shaped eyes had wings and were flying through the air.

"Skylar," he interrupted. "I think we're being followed."

She glanced back. "Spyballs!"

Skylar flapped towards the winged eyeballs, pecking at them with her beak. The flying eyes buzzed away.

"This doesn't surprise me," said Skylar. "No doubt these are the queen's spies. A week ago, Dalton and I thought we caught sight of a pod of them swimming in the runlet, but we weren't sure at the time. Now it's clear that she has eyes everywhere. In the water and the sky. We'll have to be careful what we say."

Aldwyn realized that he wasn't the only one who had encountered the spying eyeballs down by the runlet. Spyballs – what fitting names they had, he thought, given their menacing stares.

The gap between the river and the trees shrunk, and soon it was unmistakable that they had entered the Weed Barrens. Dead trees and thorny vines stretched further than the eye could see. Aldwyn wasn't scared of ghosts, but there was something about the way the wind moaned through the tree limbs that made his ear hairs stand on end. The dense, rotted undergrowth was teeming with centipedes, millipedes, billipedes and crawlers with too many legs to count. It looked as if the weeds had strangled the life out of a once vibrant forest, leaving it uninhabitable to all but the least appealing and, according to Gilbert, least tasty bugs.

"Why would anyone decide to live here?" asked Gilbert.

"Some people don't want to be found," said Skylar. "Agdaleen was born to the driftfolk, but went mad before she even got her first tattoo. At the age of six, she burned her family's wagon and all the others in their caravan to the ground. She was sent away to have her mind cleansed by the keepers of the Pineland Asylum."

"Never heard of it," said Gilbert.

"That's because she burned that to the ground too. She ran away into the night and came here."

As Aldwyn stepped over some stinkweed and around a tangle of bleeding creepers, green vines that dripped drops of red, he found himself face to face with a horrible sight: a human hand dangling by a strand of dirty yarn from a branch. An army of ants poured out from a hole between two fingers carrying their eggs. Aldwyn shuddered. Then he looked around and saw that the horrific hand wasn't the only thing hanging from the trees. Wooden doll's heads, rusty spoons and cracked mirrors were swaying slowly in the breeze. Gilbert hopped up next to Aldwyn, pressing against his side.

"We're getting close now," said Skylar, seemingly not bothered by the spooky objects.

As the group continued forwards, Aldwyn found it difficult to walk with Gilbert bumping into him constantly.

"Gilbert, could you give me a little space here?"

"Sorry."

Gilbert hopped back by about an inch, which didn't really help.

After another twenty steps, a hut made from straw and bone came into view, its rooftop and chimney shingled with rat skulls and its walls covered in weeds. A mushroom patch with toadstools and orange fungus had been planted outside.

"That must be it," said Skylar.

There were no windows to see through and no door; only a dark entryway with strands of beads dividing inside from out.

Aldwyn realised that he'd soon be called upon to use his telekinesis to unlock the dispeller chains. He'd have to tell his fellow familiars the truth: that he was magicless. He just hoped there was another way to free their loyals.

"What do we do?" asked Gilbert. "Just go up there and knock?"

"No," said Aldwyn, who might not have had magic, but knew a thing or two about sneaking into places. Of course, his area of expertise was fish and fowl shops, not witches' dens. "We wait for the right moment."

"We don't have time for that," said Skylar.

"Then we create one ourselves," replied Aldwyn. "Stay right here."

He dashed back into the tangle of rotted undergrowth and grabbed a clump of foul-smelling stinkweed in his teeth. He then returned to Skylar and Gilbert, with his eyes now watering from the horrible odour. Aldwyn spat the mouthful of weeds to the ground.

"Yeuch," he groaned, as he tried to wipe the taste from his tongue with his paw. "Skylar, drop this down the chimney. That should get the old witch out of her hut in a hurry."

"Very clever," said Skylar, nodding in approval.

She picked up the stinkweed in her claws and flew for the rooftop. As she soared over, she dropped it down the chimney. The blue jay circled back and landed beside Aldwyn and Gilbert.

"Won't be long now," said Aldwyn. "It's like leaving a skunk's tail in a butcher's shop." Skylar and Gilbert both looked at him, puzzled. Aldwyn immediately realised his mistake. "It's an expression we telekinetic cats use," he said, forcing a smile.

Just then, a figure emerged from the dark, parting the beads and limping out into the mushroom patch: this was Agdaleen. The old crone's face was hidden by a nest of grey hair that looked as if it hadn't been combed for a hundred years. She waved her bony hands in front of her nose, coughing. She muttered something under her breath before disappearing into the dead woods.

"Now's our chance," said Aldwyn.

The three didn't hesitate, knowing that they had precious little time. When they reached the entryway, Aldwyn saw that what looked like white beads from a distance were actually teeth, human and animal.

Inside, a large black cauldron bubbled in the centre of the room, a fire crackling beneath it. Clear glass jars lined the shelves, filled with every ingredient needed for concocting witches' brews: goats' tongues, mugwort, vulgar cinquefoil and goblin toes. Whole pickled groundhogs floated eerily in beet juice, their expressions frozen in terror. Leather-bound tomes were left all around, their pages stained and wrinkled from being splashed and dripped upon. Aldwyn tried not to let the creepy surroundings and the lingering foul smell of the stinkweed distract him from the fact that Jack was somewhere close by.

"There's another room," Skylar called out from up ahead. "They must be back there."

Aldwyn and Gilbert hurried over to Skylar, eager to rescue the wizards and get out of there. But to their dismay, all they discovered was Agdaleen's sparsely furnished bedroom.

Jack, Marianne and Dalton were nowhere to be found.

"Where are they?" asked Gilbert.

"You tell us," replied Skylar. "It was your puddle vision."

"Maybe she moved them," said Gilbert desperately.

"No, I don't smell Jack's scent," said Aldwyn. "He was never here."

"Are you sure you heard that pond say 'grey hair witch?'" asked Skylar accusingly.

"Yes, I'm absolutely positive," answered Gilbert. "I think."

"Why did we ever listen to you?" said Skylar, shaking her head. "You and your stupid puddle viewings. You never get them right."

Gilbert shrank back at Skylar's unkind words. It was clear that he felt terrible.

"I'm sure it was an honest mistake," said Aldwyn, trying to comfort the guilt-ridden frog. "Now let's get out of here before the old hag comes back."

The trio returned to the other room – and nearly leaped out of their skins when they saw the grey-haired witch standing beside the cauldron. She flicked her stringy hair from her eyes to reveal a thin face covered in hideous tattoos. They looked as if she had etched them herself, perhaps with her fingernails and most definitely without the aid of a mirror. She stared at the intruders, licking her dry, cracked lips.

"Lucky me," said Agdaleen in a voice that had gone scratchy from a lifetime of breathing in cauldron fumes. "Usually, I have to go hunting for ingredients." She gestured to a rack of dried frog legs and bird talons.

The familiars made a run for it, but Agdaleen was quick. She stomped down her sandalled foot, screeching out an ancient, evil chant: "*Slikts ieeja augt dervis!*"

A wall of weeds spread across the entrance, blocking Aldwyn, Gilbert and Skylar's escape.

Agdaleen cocked her head, staring intently at Skylar. "Bird, where did you get that? Your anklet."

Aldwyn hadn't given a second thought to the jewel anklet since he had first spied it upon meeting Skylar in Stone Runlet. Why the lace of silver and emerald squares was of interest to this old witch was most curious.

"I don't abide by the rules," said Agdaleen. "I'll kill you just the same."

Aldwyn glanced to Skylar, who appeared to understand the witch's words far better than he did. What did this all mean?

"Now into the pot with you!" cackled Agdaleen.

She grabbed a beaker stuffed with octopus intestines and flung it into the cauldron. The iron pot shook and eight fleshy black tentacles sprang from its outer surface. The octopot was quick to lash out. Two of its arms reached for Aldwyn, while another tried to swipe Skylar out of the air. Gilbert hopped behind a shelf for cover as three more arms slithered towards him.

"Oh yes, oh yes!" said Agdaleen as she watched the fun unfold. "Cat's paw, bird's beak, frog's legs. You should make a most delicious stew."

Aldwyn tried to defend himself as one of the octopot's tentacles wrapped itself around his tail. He had heard the old saying that a cat has nine lives, but he had no intention of finding out if it was true. He scratched viciously at the attacking arm, but whatever had been born from Agdaleen's spell seemed immune to feline claws. Across the room, Gilbert had wedged himself into a distant corner, but the octopot's reach was too great. It tossed aside the wooden shelves as if they were made of paper, closing in on the frightened frog. Meanwhile, up above, every time Skylar tried to utter the words of a spell, a rubbery arm covered her beak.

"Let go of me," shouted Aldwyn as he was pulled up off his feet and into the air. He looked down and saw that he was now dangling over a boiling broth. "On second thoughts, I take that back. Do *not* let go of me."

The tentacle began to shove Aldwyn down towards the scalding and bubbling stew, ready to dunk him under. Aldwyn gripped the edge of the pot. It was hot to the touch, but singed paws were better than being cooked alive!

With nowhere to hide, Gilbert was bouncing as fast he could across the room, ducking and dodging the swinging arms.

"I could use a little help here," he called out to his companions.

"I know what you mean," screamed Aldwyn. His claws scraped against the sides of the octopot

Skylar had dug her claws into one of the ceiling beams but a high reaching tentacle was still wrapped around her wing and beak, trying to wrestle her free.

Agdaleen picked up a firepoker and walked over to the cauldron's side, where Aldwyn was clinging on for dear life.

"You're going to taste good with a little salt and pepper," she said as she swung the poker down on Aldwyn's paws.

He winced from the blow and only just managed to hold on. His hind legs burned as boiling bubbles burst below him. Agdaleen tried pushing him in with the poker's sharp edge, but Aldwyn shifted his weight just before it hit. Instead the poker pierced Jack's pouch, which was still hanging from Aldwyn's shoulder. Aldwyn looked through the hole in the bag and spotted among the ground glow-worm and steel marbles a fistful of clovers, mostly the four-leafed variety, but a three-leafed one was shoved in there, too. Suddenly Dalton's warning to Jack during their walkabout rang in his memory: *You're only supposed to take the ones with four leaves. Anything less can curse a whole spell.*

Aldwyn's eyes lit up and his attention immediately focused on the single three-leafed clover buried at the bottom of the pouch. He stretched his neck and managed to pluck it out with his teeth. Then he exhaled, blowing it from his mouth down to the potion.

"Please work, please work, please work," he hoped aloud.

But before the clover reached the mustard-coloured liquid, a bubble of steam popped and blew it against the inside wall of the cauldron, where it got stuck. Aldwyn's eyes went wide: "No!"

He reached out his front paw, but the clover was

just too far away. Another tentacle came and grabbed him around his neck, attempting to force him into the stew. Agdaleen had turned her attention to Skylar, swinging her poker wildly at the bird, who was being suffocated by one of the pot's arms as she fluttered back and forth, trying to escape. Gilbert played leapfrog over the swinging arms, but it was clear he was growing tired.

Aldwyn stretched out his tail as far as he could until the very tip touched the three leaves of green. In Bridgetower, a street cat had to learn to use all four of their paws with equal skill, but the truly smart ones trained their tails, too. With one strained flick he sent the clover into the cauldron, and this time it landed squarely in the broth.

In an instant, the yellow liquid turned bright blue and began swirling counter-clockwise. The tentacles that had sprouted from Agdaleen's spell let go of Aldwyn, released Skylar and stopped their pursuit of Gilbert as well. It only took Aldwyn a moment to climb over the cauldron's edge and leap to freedom. Then something unexpected happened. The octopot turned its deadly attack on Agdaleen. With alarming speed, the thick arms closed around the old witch's ankles and wrists.

"What's going on?" she squealed, with panic and disbelief. "I command you, release me at once!"

Aldwyn, Skylar and Gilbert watched as she was lifted off the ground and the tentacles dragged her kicking and screaming over the cauldron.

"How dare you disobey me!" screamed Agdaleen.

The octopot's tentacles dunked the crone headfirst into the scalding soup, and as her grey hairs melted from her scalp, she let out a terrifying wail. Within seconds, only her sandalled feet stuck out above the whirlpool of boiling broth. And that's when Aldwyn noticed it: around her bony, shrivelled ankle there was a silver and emerald anklet identical to Skylar's. It disappeared into the pot before the others could see.

The weeds blocking the lair's entryway fell to the ground and the three familiars didn't wait to see what would happen next. They beat a hasty retreat and no one said a word until the straw-and-bone hut was just a dot in the distance.

"What was that all about back there?" Aldwyn asked

Skylar, finally breaking the silence. "That business about your anklet?"

"I don't know," she replied. "It was given to me as a gift when I graduated from the Aviary."

Aldwyn wasn't certain he believed her, and for a moment considered mentioning what he had seen on Agdaleen's ankle. But if he confronted Skylar about her lies, then he might be confronted about his own. So he stayed quiet.

"I'm afraid we're left with no choice but to travel to the Ocean Oracle," said Skylar. "It is a long and dangerous trek to get there, but I don't know who else has the certainty of vision to tell us where to find our loyals?"

"Well, there is somebody closer," said Gilbert, a bit reluctantly. "But he scares me even more than Agdaleen did."

Aldwyn and Skylar both looked at him.

"My dad."

NINE

The Tree Frogs of Daku

It turned out Gilbert wasn't exaggerating. He was truly terrified of his dad. All the way from the edge of the Weed Barrens to the nameless marshes through which they were now walking, Aldwyn and Skylar had listened to how Gilbert's demanding, perfectionist father had always criticised him, starting with the crooked gills he was born with as a tadpole. Gilbert went on to tell how every parent of a tree frog raised in the swamps of Daku had high hopes for their young, but none had higher expectations than his own father, the clan leader and master seer.

"And as if it wasn't bad enough having a dad who made me feel terrible about the mistakes I made," said Gilbert, "he would scold me for stuff I hadn't even done yet!"

"I guess that's one of the disadvantages of having a parent who can see into the future," said Aldwyn.

"That does sound unfortunate, Gilbert. I can see why you wouldn't want to return," Skylar said. "So, how quickly can we get there?" she added, cheery and upbeat.

Gilbert scrunched up his face, squirming with dread.

"Don't give me that look. If your father is as wise as you make him out to be, we just might have a chance of saving Dalton, Jack and Marianne yet," said Skylar.

"I know, I know," Gilbert said. "You're right."

As the sun dropped towards the horizon, the day turning to late afternoon, and the familiars travelled further, the ground became more moist with every step. Aldwyn's pace slowed, he was unable to walk as briskly and his paws were dripping with heavy, foul-smelling mud. He more than once found himself knee deep in peat bog, a sure sign that the swamplands were close.

"Home sweet home," said Gilbert with what sounded like genuine nostalgia as he happily inhaled the scent of swamp grime and mildew

Swarms of mosquitoes had begun to follow the familiars. While Gilbert was lapping up mouthfuls of them, Aldwyn couldn't keep them away and soon was covered in bites, most of them on his hind quarters.

It wasn't long before the murky waters became so deep that Gilbert, Aldwyn and Skylar had to climb aboard a log floating in the swamp. The familiars paddled with a stick past some muck vines and four chameleon crabs building a dam out of tree branches. Aldwyn recognised the magical crabs from the shopkeeper's demonstration during his brief stay in the familiar store. The three animals continued towards two swamp cypress trees that Gilbert said marked the entrance to the frog village where he had once lived.

"My brothers and sisters and I used to play hide and seek right over there," said Gilbert, pointing to the muck below the trees. "They never were able to find me. Of course now that I think about it, I'm not sure they ever bothered looking."

"Did you have many brothers and sisters?" asked Aldwyn.

"No, we were a small family. There were just the sixty-two of us."

As they steered closer to the cypress archway that welcomed visitors to Daku, two slender hunks of wood glided out from beyond the hanging vines. Each was guided by a pair of tree frogs carrying bamboo spears.

"They're friendly, right?" asked Aldwyn, cautiously eyeing the armed amphibians.

"Aldwyn, these are my people," said Gilbert with a smile. "Of course they are."

As Gilbert spoke one of the frogs sent a bamboo spear flying through the air, straight towards the familiars.

Aldwyn dived for cover, tackling Skylar and Gilbert out of the way, nearly pushing them into the water.

"I don't know what your definition of friendly is," said Aldwyn to Gilbert, "but that's certainly not mine!"

Gilbert pointed behind them and Aldwyn turned to see that the spear had killed a poisonous water snake that had been sliding along the back of their log.

"OK, forget what I said. I'm just not very good with pointy things flying towards me, that's all."

The two frog-helmed boats approached, flanking them on either side.

"Sorry about the scare," said one of the frogs. "Those snakes are deadly, you know. I think it was intending to swallow the pretty lady whole."

"Well, thank you for saving me," said Skylar.

"Not you," replied the tree frog. "The furry one."

It took a moment for Aldwyn to realise the frog was talking about him.

"Actually, I'm not a girl."

"Oh," said the frog, not completely convinced. "You cats all look the same."

"Anyway, welcome back, Gilbert," said a second frog. "We've been expecting you."

"Of course you have," said Gilbert, none too surprised.

The group was led beneath the cypress arch and into the village beyond, not one made up of huts and streets, but just trees and lily pads. Rounding the bend, Aldwyn's paws stopped paddling as his eyes discovered hundreds of tree frogs hanging from the reeds, jumping from branch to branch and swimming in the muddy water. A clamour of croaking surrounded them, both noisy and strangely melodic. The frogs of Daku were an incredibly athletic lot. Gilbert seemed lazy and uncoordinated in comparison.

When the familiars' log reached the shore, they were met by an excited group of thirty red-eyed frogs. A chorus of "Welcome back," "Hey, big brother," and "Gilbert!" followed.

"Aldwyn, Skylar, these are my brothers and sisters," said Gilbert. "Half of them, anyway."

An older female frog pushed through the crowd and embraced Gilbert. She wore several thin twine necklaces, each adorned with dozens of wooden charms.

"My baby," she said, holding back tears. "Look at how skinny you are."

"Hi, Mum," said Gilbert.

"We've missed you so much," she said.

"You and Dad?" asked Gilbert hopefully.

"*I've* missed you so much," she corrected herself. Aldwyn watched a hurt look cross Gilbert's face. "I wear your birth charm close to my heart every day." She touched one of the wood chips hanging from her neck, with a carving of a circle with a star in it. "Now come on, I have a feast waiting for you and your friends. I've been preparing it for over a week."

Aldwyn tried to wrap his head around how strange this all was, the way these frogs had known they'd visit long before he had ever met Jack, set foot in Stone Runlet, or watched Kalstaff die. A week ago, all Aldwyn had foreseen of his future were back-alley brawls over scraps of meat and sleepless nights on the rooftops.

Gilbert's mum led the trio across some mossy branches to a circle of toadstools, where a feast had been laid. And not just acorn caps brimming with juicy insects, but chopped fish for Aldwyn and nuts and berries for Skylar. Aldwyn was about to stick his nose in the wooden bowl of diced minnows when Gilbert's mum interrupted him, handing him a damp fern leaf.

"That's OK," said Aldwyn. "I'll just lick myself clean when I'm through."

"Oh, it's not for the food," she replied.

Before Aldwyn could express his confusion, a swamp parakeet flew overhead, sending a splattering of bird droppings directly onto Aldwyn's shoulder. He used the wet leaf to wipe it from his fur, then turned to Gilbert, a bit upset.

"Wouldn't it have been easier for her to just tell me to get out of the way?"

"If it has been seen in a viewing, there's nothing that can be done to change it," said Gilbert. "The future has already been written. My people just get a glimpse of it."

Aldwyn found the rules of soothsaying hard to follow. What would have happened if Gilbert's mum had warned him? Would the bird dropping have still landed on him at a later moment? Or if he ducked, would he have caused ripples in time, with disastrous cosmic results? But Aldwyn's growling stomach called his attention back to the fish.

"Gilbert, have you told your friends about that glorious day when the red-haired man came to choose one among us?" asked Gilbert's mom.

"No, they're not interested, Ma," said Gilbert,

attempting to change the subject.

"Actually, I'm *very* interested," chirped Skylar.

"It was late in the afternoon, just like now," said Gilbert's mum. "He arrived on a boat that rowed itself. It was magical! The entire village gathered to see this strange human visitor. Then he spoke to us. He said he had come to Daku looking for a frog who wished to be a familiar. He asked if there were any volunteers who would be willing to leave their family and friends to become a companion to a wizard. And who was the first to leap down from the trees? My first hatched, Gil!"

Gilbert's mum planted a kiss on Gilbert's forehead. "I was so proud," she exclaimed. His cheeks quickly filled with red.

"He didn't jump, he slipped!" called out a stronger, muscular frog from nearby. "He was chasing after a ladybird."

"Phillip, that's your older brother you're talking about," snapped Gilbert's mum. "Be nice."

Gilbert got redder. Aldwyn knew his fellow familiar well enough and could see on his face that Phillip wasn't lying.

"So, who wants seconds?" asked Gilbert's mum, taking the attention off Gilbert.

Skylar leaned over and whispered to Gilbert, trying not to appear a rude guest.

"We really should speak to your father," she said. "Remember why we're here."

"You know, the Ocean Oracle isn't *that* far away," said Gilbert with a nervous stutter.

"Gilbert—"

"OK, OK." He rubbed his hands together and cleared his throat before turning to his mother. "Mum, I need to talk to Dad."

"He knows why you've come," she replied. "You can find him meditating in the Quag."

Skylar pushed aside the rest of her nuts and berries, eager to move on to the more pressing matters at hand. Aldwyn lapped up every last chunk of fish, unsure when his next meal would come.

"Thanks, Ma," said Gilbert with his mouth full.

He led Aldwyn and Skylar down a narrow mud path, past cypress boughs weighed down by colonies of tree frogs basking in the sun. They walked through a cove where young froglets practised their puddle viewing in leaves filled with dew. Finally, they crossed over a series of lily pads to an island dense with bamboo sticks, some taller than others, but each with symbols carved into the wood.

"What are these?" asked Aldwyn.

"Valour staves," replied Gilbert. "Once a tree frog has earned the respect of the village elder – my father – a stalk of bamboo is engraved with his or her symbol and planted here surrounding the Quag."

"Where's yours?" asked Aldwyn.

"I don't have one yet."

Gilbert sucked in a big lungful of air, lifted his shoulders high and hopped through the cluster of valour staves, with Aldwyn and Skylar right behind him. There on the other side, was a pool of still water. Fireflies peacefully floated above it, making the pond glow with swirls of light. On the opposite side sat an old tree frog meditating quietly. He looked like Gilbert and all his brothers, save for the fact that he was much older and had a black diamond birthmark on his back.

"Hello, Father," said Gilbert hesitantly.

Gilbert's dad just sighed. "I thought you'd grow old

and die in that magician's pet store. I still can't believe a young wizard chose *you* as her familiar."

"Well, maybe she saw something special in me," said Gilbert meekly.

"You know, I'm a grandpa now. Little tadpoles swimming around, just a few days old, already predicting the weather," said Gilbert's dad with a sneer. "You, on the other hand, couldn't see a storm coming if the rain was pouring right down on your head."

Aldwyn felt sorry for Gilbert. Not that he'd ever had the experience, but he imagined that to be told off by one's father in front of one's friends had to be about the worst thing for anybody's self-confidence. He wanted to tell the mean old frog to back off, but then thought better of it.

"You know, life isn't just about looking into the past and future," said Gilbert, too afraid to meet his father's gaze. "It's about living in the moment and appreciating what's right in front of you."

"Who filled your head with such silly notions?"

"Marianne. The cleverest person I know," said Gilbert proudly, before turning to Skylar. "No offence."

"I had hoped you would have grown up by now," said Gilbert's dad, deeply disappointed. "But I'm not sure you'll ever learn to be like one of us."

Aldwyn thought that maybe being an orphan wasn't such a bad thing after all.

Gilbert looked as if he was ready to head back out the way they'd come. But as he turned, Skylar put a wing on his shoulder and cleared her throat.

"Forgetting something?" she said to him quietly.

"Right," he said, before turning back to his dad. "Dad, we need your help. Our loyals have been kidnapped by Queen Loranella and we don't know where to find them."

Gilbert's father looked at his son, as if staring deep into his soul.

"Give me a moment to stir the waters."

Gilbert's dad picked up a nearby stick and used it to make circles in the still pool. Immediately, pictures began to take shape on the surface, but they were flashing by too fast for Aldwyn to understand. Then one image, lasting longer than the others, caught his eye: Jack, Marianne and Dalton were chained up to the same wall as in Gilbert's vision, only this time

Queen Loranella stood across from them. She was sending bolts of electricity from the tips of her fingers at Jack, but they fizzled upon making contact with his protective forcefield. Then the picture vanished as quickly as it came, blending into more pictures. Aldwyn felt a lump in his throat bigger than any hairball. Jack was in danger and there was nothing he could do.

Gilbert's dad continued to watch intently, the images reflecting in his eyes. A chorus of voices emerged from the water, their words overlapping and tumbling over each other. Then the pool's water went still again: the viewing was complete.

"They are being held in the dungeon of the Sunken Palace," said Gilbert's dad with a voice that was full of authority but without emotion.

"Thank you so much," said Skylar. "I don't know how we can ever repay you."

"But there is a guardian," the old frog continued. "The seven-headed Hydra of Mukrete stands in the way. If you wish to make it safely past you'll need to put the beast to sleep with a special powder that can only be ground by the Mountain Alchemist."

Aldwyn sneaked a look at Skylar and Gilbert. He

wasn't surprised to see that Gilbert was frightened by what his father said, but to find Skylar staring blankly into space with equal fear made him realise just how daunting the quest was that lay ahead. Saving their loyals seemed more impossible than ever.

"You should go now," said Gilbert's dad. "The pool has no more to reveal to me. How this will all end is up to the three of you."

And with that, the old frog turned his back to the group, not even saying goodbye to Gilbert as he resumed his meditation. Aldwyn could see that Gilbert was hurt, but now was not the time to make things better between father and son.

Aldwyn, Skylar and Gilbert left the Quag and passed back through the main village.

"I know that must have been hard for you," said Skylar. "But it had to be done."

"You did good, Gilbert," said Aldwyn, giving his companion a pat on the back.

The tree frog brightened slightly, but his father's coldness had left him looking weary.

Gilbert couldn't leave without saying a final farewell to his mum. He found her sitting in a leaf hammock rocking a tadpole in her arms and singing it a lullaby.

"*Hiding high up on its head, draped in white shimmering gown, lie the keys to the past, in the snow leopard's crown,*" she whispered to a soft melody.

"Ma, I gotta go," said Gilbert quietly, trying not to disturb the baby frog.

"Do you remember when I used to sing this to you?" she asked, clearly not picking up on the urgency in his voice. "You would fall asleep in my arms even when you were a full-grown frog."

"Mum, not now," said Gilbert, embarrassed.

"I think the songbirds used to sing us the same one at the Aviary," said Skylar, remembering. "Only when I was little of course."

"I packed you some flies for the road," said Gilbert's mum, handing Gilbert a sack made from a hollowed-out flower bud. He looked inside and saw that it was stuffed with gnats and maggots. She then turned to Skylar and Aldwyn. "Take care of him. And make sure he washes his feet twice a day—"

"We're leaving," said Gilbert, cutting her off. "I love you."

He gave his mum a hug, slipped the grass straps attached to the flower bud over his shoulders like a backpack and the three familiars set off again. When they reached the mud near the log they had floated in on, Phillip was waiting.

"So long, Gilbert," said his bigger and stronger younger brother. "We'll be keeping an eye on you in the waters."

Phillip laid down a leaf over the mud and gestured for Aldwyn to cross it to the log.

"Ladies first," he said.

"I'm a boy!" exclaimed Aldwyn. "What is it with you frogs?"

Then his ears perked up at the sound of feet splashing through water. They weren't the light footsteps of tree frogs, either.

Up ahead, running through the knee-deep waters beneath the cypress archway, were a half dozen of the queen's soldiers, led by the one with the battleaxe that the familiars knew all too well. His lightning-singed scalp was unmistakable.

"How did they find us?" asked Gilbert in a panic.

The question was answered when Aldwyn spotted

a spyball flying alongside one of the guards. The winged eye stared at the familiars.

"By the order of the queen," growled the half bald soldier, "you are to come with us at once."

The guards pulled their swords, ready to take the familiars by force.

Then, from the trees, it started raining frogs. A hundred of Gilbert's brothers, sisters and cousins leaped from the foliage, bearing sharpened bamboo spears and bolas made of vine and rock. Before the soldiers knew what had hit them, they were attacked from all sides.

"Engage hand-to-hand combat," ordered Phillip, who had leaped to a nearby branch and was now hanging upside down.

The tree frogs were tiny but fearsome warriors, amphibian assassins with acrobatic skills and deadly precision. It was evident to Aldwyn that this was an orchestrated attack, one that could have only been planned with foreknowledge.

Phillip dropped to the ground and barked another command to his troops: "Full-scale assault!"

In a flash, two soldiers went face down in the

water. Their helmets had been pulled from their heads by the first wave of frogs and then they were knocked unconscious by hundreds of tiny stones launched from slingshots.

"Let's go!" shouted Gilbert to Aldwyn and Skylar. "They've got our backs."

Aldwyn and Skylar raced for the log, but the soldier carrying the battleaxe was closing ground on them quickly. There was no way they could make it. He was coming too fast.

"Aldwyn, do something!" shouted Skylar. "Use your telekinesis."

Aldwyn didn't know what to say. It was proving awfully difficult to tell Skylar and Gilbert he had no talent whatsoever, especially in these moments of crisis when his fellow familiars were counting on him.

The soldier ploughed on towards them, axe raised overhead.

"What are you waiting for?" asked Gilbert.

"I've never done this running through swamp water before," said Aldwyn desperately. "It throws off my mental balance completely."

Then, something miraculous happened: a branch

on the ground began to lift on its own, directly in the path of the charging soldier. Skylar, Gilbert and Aldwyn all watched in awe. Aldwyn couldn't believe what was happening. The guard couldn't slow down fast enough. He tripped over the floating wooden branch and fell flat on his face.

The familiars took their chance and ran for the log. Reaching it safely they began pushing it into the water.

"You did it!" exclaimed Gilbert.

"You didn't have to wait until the very last second, you know," said Skylar. "But a success all the same I suppose."

Aldwyn was amazed himself. He certainly didn't think he was responsible for the levitating branch. And then his doubts were confirmed, when he saw the true cause of his "telekinesis". Four chameleon crabs were carrying the tree branch along the edge of the water towards the dam they were building. They had been invisible just moments earlier due to their temporary camouflage spell. And lucky for Aldwyn, Skylar and Gilbert were too busy paddling the log across the mud to notice the now visible crabs. His secret would stay a secret a little longer.

As the familiars struggled to pick up speed, the battleaxe-wielding soldier was back on his feet, heading straight for them. Once again, he lifted his weapon over his shoulder, but before he could strike, the double-sided blade was ensnared in vines and yanked from his hand. The three looked back to see who was disarming their attacker – Gilbert's father!

"Dad?" Gilbert gasped, surprised to see him in the fray.

"Go," the old frog said. "Your loyals need you."

Aldwyn and Gilbert paddled as fast as they could, and their swamp vessel moved away from the scene of the battle. Behind them, Gilbert's dad swung his bamboo fighting stick. He was defending Gilbert and the other familiars with fierce paternal protection, striking the soldier in a flurry of painful blows to the throat. Watching him, Aldwyn reconsidered his earlier judgement about being better off as an orphan. Once again he longed to know his own father and mother.

As the army of tree frogs overwhelmed the rest of the soldiers, the familiars paddled off into the cool evening.

"Aldwyn, you really came through for us," said Gilbert.

Aldwyn forced a smile, knowing that his deception couldn't be maintained forever. He'd be called on to use his telekinesis again, and no chameleon crabs would be around to bail him out. Perhaps next time, Jack's life would hang in the balance.

"Yeah, you really saved the day," added Skylar. "Just in the nick of time, too."

There was something in the way she said that last part that made Aldwyn think she wasn't totally convinced.

They kept paddling, watching as the sky changed colour. The sun was setting and only two days remained before Kalstaff's protective spell would fade, leaving their loyals defenceless against the evil queen.

TEN

Vastia's Most Wanted

The tip of the enchanted quill glided across the parchment, filling in forests, gorges and deserts alongside the previously drawn map to the Weed Barrens. Aldwyn watched as Scribius inked in the words Peaks of Kailasa above a cluster of mountaintops, and Sunken Palace in the low grasslands at the top of the page. The familiars had steered their log ashore at the first sign of dry land, and here on the banks of the Daku swamp they sat, beneath the early evening moonlight, charting a new course after their hurried getaway.

"Well done, Scribius," said Skylar as she examined the path set out for them in black and white.

Aldwyn glanced over her shoulder at the parchment and realised just how far the lands of the queendom stretched.

"Wow," he said. "Vastia sure is... vast."

"We'll continue north and look for a bridge or a shallow place to walk across the river," said Skylar, drawing the tip of her wing along the wrinkled creases of the parchment and then stopping before a tri-peaked mountain at the centre of the cluster. "The Mountain Alchemist resides here, high in the Peaks of Kailasa. Long ago, he fought against the Dead Army beside Kalstaff and Loranella. Back then he had a name: Yonatan McCallister, grandson of the great diviner, Parnabus McCallister. Yonatan was wizarding royalty, a five-times champion of the Warlock Trail and undefeated in dozens of disenchantment duels. But after he was blinded during the Uprising he became a recluse. He has lived alone ever since, more interested in matters of the Tomorrowlife than the politics of Vastia. He chose to abandon his given name and is now known simply as the Mountain Alchemist."

"Then why would he help us?" asked Gilbert.

"I'm not sure that he will," she answered. "But we've got to get that sleeping powder and unfortunately he's the only one who can brew it."

Aldwyn tapped his paw impatiently as Scribius completed the map with a final flourish. Then the animal trio set off on the next leg of their journey.

Gilbert took in one last whiff of home and looked back at it fondly as he left the swamp behind for a second time. Aldwyn, however, was relieved they were on the move again: he wouldn't miss the stench or the chiggers that had been nipping at his ankles since their arrival. It wasn't all bad, though: seeing where Gilbert came from had allowed him to get to know his new friend better. At the same time, it made him realise how much remained a mystery about Skylar.

Off they went, with the black night sky serving as their ally, hiding them from whatever predators were lurking on the windswept plains. And while they didn't come face to face with any of the wild inhabitants of these badlands, they certainly felt their presence. At one point they stepped into what appeared to be a small crater, only to realise it was a footprint so large a cow could have fitted inside. They all wondered if this was the imprint of a fully grown gundabeast. If it was, it would take more than the Council's beast tamers to push it back to the Beyond.

Later, they crossed a long path of burnt and crushed grass that looked like the aftermath of fire and a stampede of hooves racing out of control. Skylar recognised the trail as that of the lightmares, a noble breed of horses that lived far in the east, high in the Yennep Mountains. They made rare visits to Vastia when they felt cracks forming in the magic energy of the land. When, a little later, Skylar heard the distant wail of a wolverine pack on the hunt, she told Aldwyn and Gilbert that it would be wise to quicken their pace, given the vicious carnivores' supernaturally enhanced sense of sight, smell and hearing. Queen Loranella's job was to keep Vastia safe, but the lands were clearly more dangerous than ever. Could this be another part of her evil plan?

It wasn't long before the familiars were staring down at the colossal body of the Ebs once more. This was a different portion of the river, and to Aldwyn's eye, the swath of clear blue water was many times broader than it had been in the south. No manmade bridge could stretch across the river Ebs here, but they had to cross it. Beyond the wide belt of blue, far away in the distance, towered the Peaks of Kailasa, their white caps reaching up to scratch the sky. Somewhere in those mountains, they would find the Mountain Alchemist, who was as yet unaware of the vital part he would play in saving Vastia once again.

"I don't suppose the two of you are up for a swim," said Skylar.

Aldwyn's eyes opened wide. He had traipsed through the sewers of Bridgetower for scraps of chicken that had washed down the drains, but as far as he was concerned, swimming in water was not what cats were made for. Crossing the Ebs would have been a daunting task even for a skilled swimmer. Gilbert, too, looked nervous, even though he had spent his childhood breathing underwater.

"The current would carry us straight out to sea,"

said Gilbert. "That's assuming the river dragons don't eat us first."

Skylar reconsidered. "OK, so maybe that was a bad idea."

Aldwyn scanned the moonlit river for another way. A safer way. A saner way. A moment later, he had spotted the solution.

"You may not have to get wet after all," he said to Gilbert. "Look out there."

Skylar and Gilbert saw where Aldwyn's paw was pointing: right in the middle of the river was a raft the size of a house. Horses and people stood atop its wooden planks as it drifted slowly through the darkness towards the far shore.

"We need to find out where that ferry left from," said Aldwyn.

They began walking once more, this time hugging the coast until they arrived at the outskirts of a town consisting of no more than a dozen buildings. The isolated trading village sat on a peninsula of land. The Ebs River flowed by on the west; to the east, it branched off into a smaller tributary, the Enaj, which stretched through the less travelled flatlands on Vastia's border.

As the trio continued to follow the river into the town, they came upon a small landing where the large wooden raft could be pulled up against the shore for loading and unloading. A timber ticket booth stood empty now with a sign propped up against its shuttered window: "Ferry Crossing – Next Raft Departs at Sunrise."

They looked out at the ferry, growing smaller as it sailed towards an unseen port on the other side.

"Let's find a safe place to sleep until morning," said Skylar. "Then we can return here for the day's first passage."

Lanterns lighted the way to the little settlement's centre. Aldwyn, Skylar and Gilbert followed the lit path between a tannery smelling of dried hides and a cobbler's shop with boots and shoes displayed in the window. The unpainted buildings looked like they had been built quickly. When the group emerged onto the town's main thoroughfare, an unpaved dirt road, Gilbert let out a terrified shriek. Aldwyn spun around to see Queen Loranella, standing tall and motionless before them. Aldwyn froze – but then immediately relaxed again: this was not her evil majesty in the flesh. No, this was a mere tapestry of the queen, woven with loving detail, but lifeless nonetheless. It was hanging on the outside wall of a small inn.

"Look at how kind and peaceful she appeared to be then," said Skylar.

"I don't care how nice she looks, she gives me the willies," said Gilbert.

"Well, a portrait of her isn't going to hurt us," replied Skylar. "In fact, this seems like a good place to spend the night. The roof sticks out far enough should it begin to rain, and we'll be protected from the wind as well."

"Sleep here? Under *her*?" asked Gilbert. "Are you crazy? No way. I don't care how warm and sheltered we are."

Aldwyn agreed. Although Gilbert's fear was irrational, there was something unsettling about cosying up beneath Queen Loranella's image when she had Jack in her grip.

Looking around, he spied a pet-sized entrance cut into the wall beside the inn's front door, big enough for a cat or a small dog to pass through. A leather flap covered the hole.

"This looks welcoming," said Aldwyn, gesturing to the animal entryway.

He stepped up and pawed aside the flap for a look inside. Skylar and Gilbert peered in next to him. This wasn't one of the finer lodgings, like those Aldwyn had scavenged through in Bridgetower. It was plain and simple. But sometimes plain and simple was all that was needed. A woman sat behind the counter reviewing a ledger, while an elderly man, most likely her husband, sat in a large chair before a crackling fire. A set of stairs led up to the rooms.

"Before we go in there, I think it's important to remember that we're being hunted by the queen," said Skylar. "No one can know our true identities. We must pose as common animals, magicless and ordinary."

Skylar didn't realise how absurd her suggestion sounded to Aldwyn. She was asking him to pretend to be the cat he really was.

"Although it's going to be difficult," continued Skylar, "we need to portray ourselves as street vermin, both uneducated and foolish." She gave a glance over to Gilbert and his bulging eyes. "Then again, maybe it won't be so difficult for you."

"Very funny," said Gilbert, none too amused by her teasing.

As they prepared to push through the flap, Aldwyn noticed that Skylar was slouching, bending over awkwardly.

"What are you doing?" he asked.

"Poor posture," she replied. "Makes me look more common."

Aldwyn had to keep himself from rolling his eyes.

The familiars entered the inn's lobby, where the elderly man was mid-conversation with the woman. "The carpet trader staying in room three said his entire wagon got swallowed whole. Said if he hadn't jumped off when he did, he would have been eaten, too. Thought it was a sandtaur."

"That's the third border monster sighting this week," replied the woman.

"Last time things from the Beyond were trespassing into Vastia, I was just a boy. That was right before the Dead Army Uprising."

"I'm sure the queen has everything under control," said the woman.

"*Miaow*," purred Aldwyn, trying to get their attention. He put on his most appealing and wide-eyed face. "*Miaow.*"

The woman peeked over her glasses and stared down at Aldwyn standing on the floor before her.

"Oh my," she said sweetly. "Aren't you adorable!" Then she gave a sideways glance to Skylar and Gilbert. "And what strange company you're keeping." She turned to the stairs and called, "Tammy! You've got some playmates here."

After a moment, an orange and white plains cat came down the steps. She was slightly smaller than Aldwyn, with hazel eyes and a curvy tail. Aldwyn's eyes went even wider.

"Well, hello there," said the cat with a friendly smile. "I'm Tammy. You're certainly travelling late tonight. Where are you folks from?"

Skylar and Gilbert just stood there; clearly neither were experienced in lying. Aldwyn came to the rescue.

"Oh, we met up along the main road yesterday. Decided to join together, for there is safety in numbers. A small animal alone out there is putting himself in a lot of danger. Skylar here got separated from her flock, migrating towards the mountains. Gilbert is collecting flies to take back to his family in the swamps. And me, I'm just a regular alley cat from Bridgetower. I got chased out of town by a ruthless bounty hunter. I've been on the run ever since."

"Well, you'll be comfortable here," said Tammy, clearly taking a liking to Aldwyn. "Follow me out to the barn."

Aldwyn, Skylar and Gilbert all exchanged a quick glance before heading back out through the flap, right behind Tammy.

"Very convincing," Skylar complimented Aldwyn with a whisper. "Especially that part about you and the bounty hunter. Genius."

"Yeah, I don't know where I come up with this stuff," he replied.

Tammy walked them around the back of the inn, past a pile of furnace soot and into a large stable, where two stallions, a pink-bellied pig and a couple of chickens were already sleeping in the open stalls.

"Make yourselves comfortable," said Tammy. "The innkeeper always leaves scraps out by the back door."

"We really appreciate your help," said Aldwyn.

"There's a nest up there for you," said Tammy to Skylar, "and some haystacks and blankets over there if you like," she added to Aldwyn and Gilbert. "Now, would any of you like a cup of warm milk before bed?"

"Oh, no, dairy makes my puddle viewings foggy," said Gilbert. Skylar glared at him, shooting daggers from her eyes, and he realised his mistake. "Not that I'm a magical, soothsaying frog or anything. No, not me. I can't see the future—"

A wing muffled any further words coming out of his mouth.

"You'll have to excuse him," said Skylar. "He bumped his head when he was a tadpole."

Aldwyn turned to Tammy. "I'd love some milk," he said in his most charming voice. She smiled at him and led him out of the barn.

The two cats strolled back towards the inn beneath the stars, passing windows with snoring guests sleeping inside.

"I don't think I got your name," said Tammy.

"Oh, it's Aldwyn."

"Aldwyn, the alley cat," she purred. "All the way

from Bridgetower. So, what's it like in the big city?"

"It's a pretty dangerous place. I didn't lose this chunk of my ear chasing wool."

"Housecats like me don't see too much trouble," said Tammy, clearly thrilled by the whiff of danger. "What did you do to get run out of town?"

"I got caught stealing," said Aldwyn. "A fishmonger got wise to me and he sent the meanest bounty hunter in all of Vastia after me."

How refreshing it was to be able to speak the truth for once. Looking into Tammy's eyes, he could tell that she didn't care that he couldn't move objects with his mind or cast a spell.

"Didn't someone leave food out for you every day?" she asked.

"I wish. I've been scrapping for meals for as long as I can remember. Ever since I was a kitten."

"What about your parents?"

"I never knew them," said Aldwyn sincerely, a hint of sadness in his voice. "The streets were probably hard enough on them without an extra mouth to feed."

"Stories like that just break my heart."

"It worked out OK for me. Taught me to rely on

myself. In the end, that's really the only thing you can count on."

Tammy moved closer to Aldwyn, her fur almost grazing his. They continued on in silence for a while.

"Where are you headed from here?" Tammy asked, clearly wishing for an invitation.

"We're all taking the ferry out in the morning. Making our way to…" Aldwyn hesitated. He knew he couldn't tell her about the Mountain Alchemist or the Sunken Palace. It would put all of them at risk, including Tammy. "…Friendlier shores," he said simply.

"You've got a friend right here."

The two of them shared a smile and Aldwyn's stomach did a little somersault. Then Tammy stopped. They had walked past the inn and reached the river's edge. She looked around.

"I completely forgot what we came out here for," she said.

"Milk."

"Right. We walked clear past it. Sorry about that."

Tammy bashfully turned her head and led them back towards the inn. But Aldwyn didn't need an apology. The midnight heart-to-heart had been a welcome escape from pretending to be a familiar and worrying about Jack and the queen. In fact, he would have been happy to keep on walking.

A splash of cold water landed on his fur. Then another. He was shivering. Wet. The sound of a kitten mewling. Was it coming from him or someone else? He saw the blue, cloudless sky above him. Then he heard a voice, as if it was inside his head. Sweet and tender. "Goodbye, Aldwyn..."

"Aldwyn, Aldwyn," a female voice repeated as he was shaken out of his dream. Aldwyn's eyes half-opened and he saw Tammy standing over him. "Aldwyn, wake up."

Aldwyn could see the light shining in through the cracks of the barn. It was dawn, which meant that sunrise was less than an hour away. He thought back on the dream he had just been pulled from. It had been different from the recurring one he had had on the rooftop in Stone Runlet. That voice. The mewling. New mysteries for him to ponder some other time.

He got his bearings and looked up at Skylar, still sleeping in the nest, then over at Gilbert, also fast asleep, nuzzled up next to the pink-bellied pig. Tammy slid a piece of paper in front of Aldwyn.

"This was left under the door for the innkeeper," she said. "They've been posted everywhere."

Aldwyn looked down at the flyer and saw a rough but unmistakable sketch of Skylar, Gilbert and himself with the word **WANTED** written above their pictures. The text written below read:

"*Queen Loranella demands the capture of these three animals. Dead or Alive. A handsome reward will be paid directly from the Palace Vault upon the delivery of their bodies.*"

A sense of dread washed over him.

"This is all over a piece of stolen fish?" asked Tammy.

"It's a little more complicated than that. Skylar, Gilbert, we have to go. Get up!" His call was so urgent Skylar immediately popped out of the nest. Gilbert awoke more slowly, then did a double take upon finding himself cuddled up to the pig.

"Aldwyn, you can trust me," said Tammy. "I just want to help."

"I know," he replied. "But the less you know, the

better. I don't want to put you in any more danger than you're already in."

"What's going on?" Skylar fell silent when she saw the poster. Gilbert started complaining about not really being as fat as the picture made him look, but Tammy interrupted him. "What is this all about?"

Aldwyn gave in. They needed all the help they could get. He quickly recounted the last two days' events to Tammy – how they were familiars searching for their loyals, how the queen and her soldiers attacked them in Stone Runlet, and how they had less than two days to reach the Sunken Palace before it was too late. Her eyes grew bigger and bigger with every added detail. When he had finished, Tammy had a new look of determination in her hazel eyes. "Follow me," she said, taking control of the situation.

Tammy led them to the main road in front of the inn. It was already busy with merchants and tradesmen heading through town. More troubling was the fact that nailed to every door and horse post was the Wanted poster. With a rich bounty on their heads, Aldwyn knew that hundreds of eyes would soon be looking for them.

Sklyar was thinking along the same lines. "There's no way we can make it to the landing without being caught," she said.

Two rug merchants who had just finished reading one of the posters were walking right towards them, but before the animals could be spotted, Tammy led them into the space under the inn's raised porch and out of sight. She ducked down beside Aldwyn.

"This is all rather exciting," she said.

"Is anybody else's tongue sweating?" asked Gilbert. The others just looked back at him blankly. "OK, I guess it's just a frog thing."

Aldwyn took a breath. "Maybe we're overreacting. I mean, these aren't trained hunters. They're just carpet traders."

The words had barely passed his whiskers when a pair of black leather boots stopped right before the porch. Bronze spikes tipped the toes. Aldwyn knew these boots. He peeked out to see an ominous figure standing not eight tail lengths away.

It was Grimslade, just as he had feared.

The notorious Vastian bounty hunter held the Wanted poster in his hand, his crossbow at the ready.

Aldwyn should have known that Grimslade would not be able to resist such a prize, such a challenge, but how could he have tracked them all the way here? And so quickly? Unless, of course, the posters were already in Bridgetower.

Skylar and Gilbert had by now also taken a peek at the claw-scarred man cloaked in black.

"He looks a lot meaner than the other merchants," said Gilbert.

"That's because he's no merchant," said Skylar. "He's a bounty hunter."

Aldywn wondered how she knew. But he didn't even have to ask for an explanation.

"See that dangling from his waist," she said to the others. "It's an Olfax tracking snout."

There, hanging by a gold chain, was a wolf's nose that had been sliced clean off the face of its unfortunate owner. The nostrils were sniffing the air, as if following the scent of its game. No doubt this forbidden tool was another of the bounty hunter's illegal purchases from the Sewer Markets, like the shadow hound before. A moment later, the bronze-tipped boots walked up the steps of the inn and entered the building, mistakenly following the snout onto the porch, not under it.

"We should make a run for the ferry," said Skylar.

"We'll never make it," said Aldwyn. "Not with all these people out here looking for us."

Then Tammy spoke up: "I've got an idea. Let's get back to the barn."

The four of them made a dash back towards the barn. On the way to the stable doors, Tammy had them stop by the pile of furnace soot and ordered Aldwyn to roll around in it. Aldwyn immediately caught onto her plan, and he smiled: "You're a clever kitten!" He jumped right into the soot and did two rollovers. When he stood up, his fur was a light charcoal grey.

Inside the barn, Tammy turned her attention to Gilbert.

"Your disguise is going to be a little uncomfortable," she said.

Before Gilbert could protest, Tammy grabbed a bucket from the horses' trough and began covering Gilbert in a thin layer of cornmeal paste.

"Skylar, gather up some stray chicken feathers from

the coop," she said. "And Aldwyn, we could really use a carrot."

Gilbert stood there dripping in yellow sludge. He licked a little off his hand.

"Not bad," he said, shrugging.

Skylar came back and pressed feathers into the sticky cornmeal. After a few trips from the coop to Gilbert, she had succeeded. Gilbert looked like a short white chicken. Tammy placed the small carrot Aldwyn had found on the frog's nose for a beak.

"Now Skylar, you're roughly the same size as a cardinal, right?" said Tammy with a mischievous grin. "If we dunked you in tomato juice—"

"Tempting, but I think I'll fly across the river instead," Skylar said quickly.

As much as everybody would have liked her to join them in costume, she had a point. Besides, they had a ferry to catch! The now unrecognisable Aldwyn and Gilbert, along with Skylar and Tammy, stormed out of the barn and darted from building to building before coming to a stop behind the tannery. Between them and the ferry landing, where just a few passengers remained on shore waiting to board, was a wide stretch of road, a busy crossing that was sure to test if their disguises would work.

"We need to split up here," said Aldwyn. "Skylar, fly ahead without us, and Gilbert and I will meet up with you where the ferry docks on the other side of the river."

She nodded.

"I wish I could come with you," said Tammy, stepping closer to Aldwyn. "But I don't know what help I'd be. There's probably not much use on a magical mission for a regular cat like me."

Little did she know how alike they really were! Aldwyn promised himself that one day he would tell her the whole truth.

"Thank you. For everything," he said.

Tammy nuzzled his neck, getting a few specks of grey soot on her nose.

"You should hurry," Skylar said. "The last people are boarding the ferry."

"Good luck," Tammy called as Aldwyn and Gilbert stepped out onto the road.

The two moved swiftly along the path crowded with traders and their horses. Aldwyn led the way, while Gilbert tried to keep up behind him.

"Quit hopping," said Aldwyn.

"Oops," said the feathered frog, changing his bounce to a waddle. "I forgot."

Gilbert was hardly the most convincing chicken. Not only were his movements highly questionable, but the feathers on his body kept making him sneeze.

To make matters worse, now a small gang of townfolk was marching in their direction.

"The cat, over there!" a voice called out, but then the mob moved right past them.

"I saw it heading for the tavern," continued the same voice as they turned the corner.

Aldwyn relaxed. Their disguises, as makeshift as they were, seemed to be serving their purpose.

But just as they had reached the ferry landing and pushed in between a crowd of driftfolk and miners, Grimslade appeared again, led by the wolf's nose. Aldwyn looked over his shoulder and saw that the bounty hunter was homing in on them, the snout breathing excitedly and tugging at its chain. Gilbert glanced back and saw him as well.

"It's the bounty hunter," he croaked nervously.

Up ahead, dockhands were beginning to close the railing on the back of the ferry.

"The rest of you will have to wait until the high sun crossing," announced a dockhand to the remaining travellers.

"We need to get on that boat," said Aldwyn. "Run!"

Aldwyn and Gilbert burst out from between the legs of one of the driftfolk and sprinted for the raft. Behind them, Grimslade had stopped and was scanning his surroundings. The Olfax snout was sniffing wildly, a sure sign that what it was hunting had to be hiding somewhere nearby.

Aldwyn and Gilbert scurried beneath the guardrail and onto the ferry just as the dockhands finished untying the raft from the landing. Gilbert relaxed, convinced they were out of harm's way.

"We made it," he said.

"We're not safe until the boat leaves," replied Aldwyn.

A large juicy fly landed on Aldwyn's back and Gilbert shot his tongue out, slurping it up.

"Gilbert, chickens don't eat flies!"

"I'm sorry. I couldn't help myself. I haven't had breakfast yet."

Anxiously, Aldwyn glanced back at Grimslade. And he was right to be anxious, because the bounty hunter had his eyes locked on the two of them. Clearly, Gilbert's slip-up hadn't escaped his notice. Then Aldwyn saw a trail of sooty grey pawprints in the sand leading to the raft and he knew that the game was up.

"Come on, come on," said Aldwyn frantically even though he knew the dockhands couldn't understand him. "Let's go."

Now Grimslade was running down the slope towards the water, his boots kicking up mud behind him. "Stop that ferry!" he shouted.

As the raft moved further from the shore, Grimslade charged into the river. He pulled his crossbow from his shoulder and took aim at Aldwyn, firing off a steel-tipped bolt

It whizzed across the surface of the water and embedded itself in the wooden side rail, missing Aldwyn by mere inches. The boat was picking up speed now, putting a safe distance between them and Grimslade, who was wading in deeper, but to no avail. When he was up to his chest in water, the bounty hunter stopped and simply stared at Aldwyn and Gilbert, silent and menacing.

Aldwyn exhaled, relieved to have narrowly escaped capture yet again. But he was certain this would not be the last time he would find himself the target of Grimslade's deadly crossbow.

ELEVEN

The Bridge of Betrayal

Aldwyn and Gilbert sat on the edge of the raft, still disguised as a grey cat and a chicken. They stared down at the clear blue waters of the Ebs as the ferry glided towards the dock on the other side. The raft shook as a wave hit it and Aldwyn realised he hadn't felt seasick during any part of the voyage. He thought of what Jack had asked him during their bedtime conversation and couldn't wait to tell his wizard companion that he'd be well-suited to make many a long ocean journey with him into the Beyond. Aldwyn hoped Marianne didn't have a similar wish to travel the world, as Gilbert had appeared nauseous from the moment they had hit their first wave.

Two sturdy men carrying pickaxes, whose shoulders were as wide as wagon wheels, walked up to the side rail. One of them held the Wanted poster in his hand. His fingernails were crusted with silver ore.

"Animal fugitives?" he asked his fellow traveller. "What do you suspect they did? Chew up the royal slippers?"

The two let out a nasty laugh.

"The queen hasn't been right in the head for months," replied the one with the cracked boots, whose feet, Aldwyn couldn't help but notice, stank of spoiled bacon. "I heard she dismissed all the Council elders and replaced them with servants too fearful to question her."

"As long as the mines keep hiring, it don't matter to me."

Aldwyn gave Gilbert a tug and pulled him to the other side of the raft, away from the scary looking miners who would have grabbed them in a heartbeat if they realised the prize that was sitting at their feet.

As the ferryman guided the boat through the shallows, Aldwyn observed how different it was on this side of the river. A green forest came down towards them, reaching all the way to the shore. Scribius had drawn this on the map and called it the Hinterwoods. The air felt different here too, drier and filled with the smell of fallen pine needles. The Peaks of Kailasa towered behind the forest, appearing far closer than they actually were.

When the ferry reached the landing, one of the raftsmen leaped to the dock and tied the boat fast. Passengers began to unload their cargo, and Aldwyn and Gilbert darted off in the midst of the crowd. Surveying the port, Aldwyn didn't see any sign of Skylar, but he did notice two buildings, one a small shop selling mining equipment, the other a place to dine and rest, with tables and hammocks inside. A red mud road led away from the river, carving a twisting path through the Hinterwoods to the mountains.

"Hey, over here," they heard Skylar's voice call from a low-lying palm frond.

Aldwyn and Gilbert turned to see a black beak sticking out from behind the green leaves and hurried over. With Scribius's map unfolded at her feet, Skylar was busy plotting their next move.

"We'll follow the road here," she said, gesturing to a bridge on the map. "This is the only way to cross the gorge that separates us from the Peaks of Kailasa."

"It's nice to see you too," said Gilbert. But Skylar continued, ignoring him.

"Then we'll have to make our own path to the Mountain Alchemist." She looked up at them and stopped, trying to hold back a laugh. "I'm sorry, but have the two of you looked at yourselves recently?"

Aldwyn peered down to see he only had polka dots of grey left on his black-and-white fur. Gilbert fared no better: the carrot beak was hanging off his face at an odd angle and patches of green skin were visible where feathers had once been stuck.

"It was a long trip," said Aldwyn.

"Well, you won't be needing disguises where we're headed," said Skylar. "Fortunately, few dare to brave the unknown horrors that lurk in the heart of the mountains."

"Fortunately?" asked Gilbert in a state of alarm. "What's fortunate about that?"

"We should keep moving," urged Aldwyn, glancing up at the Peaks. "This looks like a steep climb."

Aldwyn's first concern was rescuing Jack and the other loyals, who were chained up in the dungeon of the Sunken Palace. But now he had Grimslade to worry about, as well. He knew full well that the bounty hunter would be travelling on the next ferry across, if he wasn't taking a different boat even sooner.

The sounds of men and horses had long faded into the distance as the familiars hiked up the red-mud road towards the mountains. Aldwyn had washed the remaining soot from his fur and Gilbert pulled every last chicken feather from his cornmeal-covered body, yelping every time he removed one.

"So when you said 'unknown horrors', what exactly did you mean?" Gilbert asked Skylar as he looked nervously to the eerily still woods on either side of the road.

"Well, if I knew what they were, they wouldn't be unknown, would they?"

Gilbert let out a gulp.

The path was getting steeper now and the air thinner. The treeline of the Hinterwoods cleared and from atop this high vantage point Aldwyn could see just how far he had come; leagues upon leagues of East Vastia spread out below them, all the way back to Bridgetower, which from here appeared to be just a dot on the Ebs. Aldwyn's eyes slowly retraced their trail along the river back to the grey and green brush of the Weed Barrens. His leg muscles still ached from the tight grip of the octopot's tentacles. Then his gaze shifted ever-so-slightly to the swamps of Daku, and he wondered if Gilbert's father was watching them right now – or rather, he corrected himself, in the future. North of Daku, past the windswept fields, was the outpost town where Tammy had allowed him to feel comfortable in his own skin again. He certainly wouldn't mind having another moonlit stroll with her at some point. Finally he glanced down to the river, where the ferry was making another crossing. How quickly a journey could be made in one's mind when the travels by foot took so long!

Gilbert, huffing and wheezing, found a spot to stop along the side of the road. He dug into his flower-bud backpack of flies and maggots that his mother had given him. Although the meal itself seemed quite unappetising to Aldwyn, the thought of a snack was tempting. He decided to search Jack's pouch, hoping to find something to eat inside. Since Agdaleen had poked a hole through the top, Aldwyn had been extra careful to keep it upright. And sure enough, not a single item had spilled from it during their trek. He pawed through the steel marbles, ground glow-worm and clover to see what might be hiding beneath them. He discovered a whittled stick, a piece of chalk and a small square of white toffee. The confection was a sugary treat for a boy but a tooth-sticking, stomach-twisting bad idea for a cat. On a previous hungry day in Bridgetower, Aldwyn had made the mistake of scraping a gob of mint toffee off the bottom of a bench and eating it. For a week after, he had a sore belly and aching teeth. He chose to leave the sweet alone, but before he tightened the strings of the pouch, he spied a folded up piece of parchment. Aldwyn gently plucked it out with his teeth and flattened it with his paw. There on the page was a picture sketched in charcoal of Aldwyn sleeping by the fire in Kalstaff's cottage. Jack must have drawn it while Aldwyn was dreaming that first evening in Stone Runlet. The words "My Familiar" were written above the drawing. This picture and those two simple words gave Aldwyn a warm tingling deep in his chest. This, he thought, is what it must feel like to be loved.

"We're going to find them," said Skylar. She put a comforting wing around his shoulder.

Aldwyn nodded before returning the parchment to the pouch.

After consulting Scribius's map once more, Skylar flew forwards, with Aldwyn and Gilbert following behind. It looked as if no human travellers had ventured this far for some time, given the lack of footprints. As they went further still, a chill wind began to cut across the slope, blowing through Aldwyn's whiskers and making it difficult for Skylar to fly. Then from above, they saw four hoofed white feet coming down the mud road. The feet belonged to a bearded billy goat, who appeared before them. He had snow on his back and icicles dangling from the fur on his chin and eyebrows.

"Are you lost?" asked the billy goat. "I don't see many who climb this high."

"We're heading for the Peaks," explained Skylar.

"I've just returned from there. A month of prayer at the very top. Are you seeking spiritual guidance as well?"

"No," replied Skylar. "We have more earthly matters to tend to."

"Have you made this trip before?"

The familiars shook their heads.

"Well, I'd be careful if I were you. It's winter up there. And a thunderstorm is already brewing. If you thought snow was bad, wait until it comes hand-in-hand with lightning."

"We won't be staying long," said Aldwyn.

"Oh, and I hope you're not planning on crossing the bridge together," the goat said, rather casually.

"It's my understanding there's no other way," said Skylar.

"There isn't," said the billy. "But it would be wise for you to travel across one by one."

"Why?" asked Gilbert in a mild panic. "It's not one of those rope bridges with the wooden planks you can fall through, is it?"

"No, it's stone and you won't easily fall off."

Gilbert gave a relieved sigh.

"Unless you're pushed," added the goat.

Aldwyn wondered if the billy's lonely time in the mountains had made him a little crazy.

"Some call it the Bridge of Betrayal. You see, after the Uprising, two captains of old Vastia, best friends from the Royal Guard, had travelled here to look for any remaining zombie soldiers of the Dead Army. They didn't find any, but they did stumble across a map buried in the snow. A treasure map."

Out of the corner his eye, Aldwyn could see from Skylar's intent gaze that this was a legend that even she had never heard.

"Unfortunately, while crossing the bridge, the friends turned on one another, both greedy for the fortune the map promised. They fought, and in their struggle, they threw each other over the side into the gorge below. Neither man nor map was ever found. Only their donkey lived to tell the tale. Since that day, the bridge has been cursed. Anyone who crosses it with others will betray their fellow travellers."

With these words, the goat picked up his slow, solitary trot down the mud road. The familiars were left to ponder his warning as they continued up the steep slope.

Within minutes, the winds got even stronger and the air colder. A dusting of snow started swirling around the bigger boulders. In the near distance, stretching across the seemingly bottomless mountain gorge, was the stone bridge. It looked majestic and quite safe, with brown brick walls as high as a man's waist. It certainly didn't appear cursed to Aldwyn.

"The wind is too strong. I can't fly," said Skylar. "I'll have to walk across the bridge as well. I'll go first. Then Gilbert. Aldwyn, you can—"

"There, nearing the bridge!" a voice called out.

Aldwyn whipped his head around to see two men dressed in leather armour, one carrying a net, the other holding a noose; and behind them, came Aldwyn's arch enemy. Just as he had feared, Grimslade had tracked them down. The assassins were charging up the hill, racing towards Aldwyn, Skylar and Gilbert.

"Go, go, go!" shouted Aldwyn.

The three familiars raced as fast as paw, foot and wing could carry them, but still the distance between themselves and their pursuers was shrinking rapidly. They arrived at the foot of the bridge. Skylar looked back at the oncoming bounty hunters, then at the long overpass of brown bricks, each stamped with a picture of a king's throne.

"We're going to have to cross the bridge together," she said.

"But what about the goat's——?" asked Gilbert, but he didn't even finish the question before Aldwyn and Skylar had started to race across. The tree frog immediately began jumping after them.

Aldwyn felt the wind pounding at his ears, all but deafening him. He could barely hear himself think. Then he heard a voice.

They know your secret. They'll expose you for who you really are.

Aldwyn stopped and turned around, but there was nobody there. Who was speaking to him?

Get rid of them. Start with the bird. She's on to you. She knows you're just an ordinary alley cat.

Aldwyn stopped again, trying to shake the crazy voice out of his head. Then he noticed that Skylar had halted in her tracks as well and she was batting at the air above her with one of her wings. More troubling, she was talking to herself.

"I don't need all the credit," she said aloud. "So what if they share in the glory?"

She paused and seemed to be listening to secret words only she could hear.

"My name alone in the history books?" she asked. "Yes, that would be nice."

She glared at Aldwyn menacingly. This was a look he had never seen from her before, and it was more than a little frightening.

Then the voice spoke to him once more.

Do it. Rid yourself of the problem. Snap her wings. Then throw her over the edge.

Aldwyn felt his paws twitch. It would be so easy. He maintained control, though, and tried to think clearly. These were his friends. Why would he hurt them?

Aldwyn had a moment of realisation: so that's why the goat called this the Bridge of Betrayal! And the voices must have been talking to Gilbert, too, because now Aldwyn could hear him shout: "Don't come any closer! These are my flies and you can't have them!"

He clutched the flower bud backpack tightly.

"Let's all calm down," said Aldwyn. "The bridge is doing this."

"Don't try your tricks on me," replied Gilbert.

Now really wasn't the best time for in-fighting. Grimslade and the other two bounty hunters were coming quickly towards them.

The familiars still had half the bridge to cross, but they were too filled with mistrust to continue.

"If I save the wizards," said a possessed Skylar, "my name will be known all across Vastia."

Now's your chance. Chuck her into the gorge...

Aldwyn took a step closer to her.

"I see both of you eyeing my maggots!" yelled Gilbert. "Well you can't have them!"

He looked like he was about to charge at his companions. Aldwyn and Skylar were moving towards each other, ready to attack. Then, from behind them, they heard the sounds of a horrible struggle. They shifted their attention to see the two assassins on the bridge with arms locked, wrestling one another. The net and the noose had been dropped.

"I'm the one who tracked them," one shouted, his voice filled with hatred. "The whole reward should be mine."

"Well, you never would have survived the trek up the mountain if it wasn't for me," replied the other.

There was no mistaking it: Aldwyn knew they were hearing voices in their heads, too. One was clearly stronger than the other, and he pushed his comrade so hard into the wall of the bridge that it knocked a few bricks into the gorge below. The bigger assassin pushed again, but this time, the smaller hunter moved quickly, grabbing the larger one's arm and flinging him over the side. Aldwyn could hear his scream as he fell to a most certain death.

This was enough to snap Aldwyn and Skylar out of the bridge's curse. Gilbert, however, was still held by its power.

"You can't have them," he screamed. "No one can."

"Gilbert, nobody wants your flies," said Aldwyn,

trying to calm the tree frog while watching the surviving assassin approach Grimslade with a bloodthirsty look in his eyes.

"Sorry, old chap," the smaller hunter said. "I think it's time for you to take a tumble as well."

"You fool," said Grimslade. "Now I'm going to have to kill you."

With an outstretched, gloved hand Grimslade seized his throat. The hunter in the chokehold reached behind him and grabbed a loose brick. He swung it across the side of Grimslade's face, knocking him to the ground.

Aldwyn, distracted by their foes' deadly fight, suddenly found two froggy hands wrapped around his own neck, feebly attempting to choke the life out of him.

"You'll never have them," cried Gilbert

Skylar flew over and tried to pull him off Aldwyn.

"Gilbert, let go," she said.

Fortunately, Gilbert wasn't a very strong frog, and Skylar and Aldwyn were able to pin him to the ground.

Aldwyn slapped a paw across his face.

"Snap out of it!"

Gilbert blinked hard.

"What happened?" he asked, suddenly himself again.

Aldwyn turned back to see Grimslade picking up the net and throwing it over the other man's head. With his opponent in a tangle, Grimslade charged at him, and the strength of his attack knocked both of them over the side. Grimslade, however, hung on to the edge of the wall with his fingers, while the other assassin caught hold of his leg just moments before plunging. He held on desperately and looked up with pleading eyes.

"I'm sorry, I never meant to betray you," the assassin said. "It was the voices."

But Grimslade was still clutching the bridge, so words of betrayal were still ringing in his head. He kicked out at his companion, sending him into the gorge.

"Come on," said Skylar to Aldwyn and Gilbert. "Let's go."

Skylar and Gilbert began hurrying across the bridge towards the snow-covered Kailasa mountainside. But

Aldwyn headed back to where Grimslade hung on for dear life, his fingers struggling to retain their hold on the stone.

"I don't suppose you'd want to lend me a paw," said Grimslade. "Seeing as how we're old friends, you and I."

It would be so easy, Aldwyn thought. A quick bite into his fingertips, a scratch to the back of his hand and the man who had been ruthlessly chasing him would no longer be a threat.

But Aldwyn was no killer. He lived by the strict code of the back alleys and taking out an enemy in this manner would not be honourable. Of course, should wind or gravity finish off the bounty hunter, well, that would not be his problem. Aldwyn turned and ran for the Kailasa mountainside.

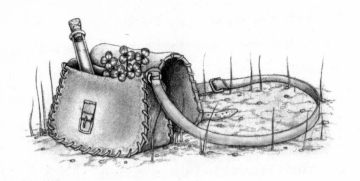

TWELVE

A Secret History

Aldwyn caught up with Skylar and Gilbert, and the three of them began climbing the Kailasa Mountains. It wasn't long before a fierce blizzard was swallowing them in a storm of white. Aldwyn glanced back as they struggled higher; the bridge could no longer be seen through the wall of snow and their footprints had disappeared under a blanket of powder.

"I can't believe I was about to betray you both

for fame," said Skylar.

"Well, it's not as bad as strangling your best friend over a bag of flies," said Gilbert. "I mean, a cat wouldn't even want flies." He paused, then turned to Aldwyn. "Would you?"

Aldwyn just shook his head.

"What were the voices saying to you?" Skylar asked Aldwyn.

Aldwyn silently took a few steps through the cold, wet snow. He couldn't tell them the truth.

"Oh, you know, typical betrayal stuff," he said. "Something about me being the new familiar and you two teaming up against me."

"Well, I hope you know that's not true," said Skylar. "We're all in this together."

The trio trudged higher. The snow was piling up and getting deeper and deeper. Once or twice, Gilbert hopped into a bank so tall that he ended up neck deep in the soft, white powder. Worse still, thunder was beginning to crackle overhead and lightning bolts were dancing from cloud to cloud.

"Lightning snow, just as the billy goat warned," said Skylar. "A rare and dangerous phenomenon. We could get fried and frozen at the same time."

"Sounds like a fun combination," said Aldwyn without even a hint of a smile.

"The chances of getting struck by lightning are one in a million," said Gilbert, trying to ease his own worries.

"Not in the mountains," replied Skylar.

Like an exclamation mark, a lightning bolt struck a nearby rock, splintering it in a flash.

Aldwyn remembered Kalstaff's words about Queen Loranella's weather binding spells and wondered if the severe storm was sent purposefully to prevent the familiars from ever reaching the Sunken Palace. One thing was for sure: the blizzard was slowing their climb to the Mountain Alchemist's hideaway.

Soon it seemed as if the three familiars weren't making any progress at all. For every step forward, they were blown two steps back. At this rate, they would find themselves back at the Bridge of Betrayal, a delay they could not afford.

"This is useless," said Skylar. "We're better off seeking shelter until the storm breaks."

Time was precious; and although it was impossible to tell through the blizzard's dark clouds, Aldwyn could sense another sunset upon them. That meant only one full day remained until Kalstaff's protective spell over Jack, Marianne and Dalton would fade. But he also knew Skylar was right. Beyond the fact that the going was slow and dangerous, the cold was turning Gilbert as blue as Skylar's feathers.

"I agree," he said. "We need to find cover somewhere."

"M-m-m-m-aybe over th-th-th-there," said Gilbert, teeth chattering. "B-b-b-b-y the r-r-r-r-rocks."

He pointed over to the hollowed-out mouth of a cave. Inside was a shelter that seemed large, wide and protected.

The familiars entered and collapsed onto the hard stone floor at the front of the cave. It was impossible to see how deep it went. Even the flashes of lightning weren't bright enough to reveal its furthest reaches. Skylar removed some nightshade, juniper berries and sage leaves from her satchel.

"What are you doing?" asked Gilbert. "You know you're not supposed to dabble with human magic."

"I'm going to conjure a fire spirit to warm us," she replied. "Otherwise, we'll all freeze to death."

"It's dangerous and forbidden," said Gilbert. "But I am losing circulation in my toes. Just cast it – I won't tell."

Skylar tossed the components into the air and chanted, "Send a flame from whence you came!" A thumb-high sprite materialised. Although she was tiny, the heat she created as she danced in the air was equal to that of a crackling bonfire.

Gilbert was the first to drift off to sleep; Skylar soon followed. Aldwyn considered keeping watch, but instead leaned his head against a silver and red rock. He figured there was little chance of another traveller making it this far, let alone finding them. Within moments, he too slipped off into a slumber and the dreams that would accompany him there.

The sound of twigs could be heard snapping. His body rocked from side to side as thunder crashed above. Then he was flipping... drowning... head to toe underwater. He came up for air, breathing once more. Tiny paw-prints in the mud. Then a sight before him: tall and white...

Aldwyn's eyes opened. This had been another new dream. Just like the journey he was on, it seemed as if his mind was travelling too, taking him places he had never been. Or had he?

It was early morning and the lightning snow had passed. Aldwyn awoke with a yawn. He tried to sit up but found himself tugged back to the floor of the cave. That was odd, he thought. Then he noticed that Jack's pouch, strapped over his shoulder, seemed to be stuck fast to the red and silver rock he had been sleeping on. There was no glue or sticky substance on the leather pouch. What was going on? Puzzled, he opened it, and the steel marbles Jack kept inside shot out, clinging to the magnetic rock.

Aldwyn shrugged and was about to wake up Skylar and Gilbert, when his attention was drawn somewhere else. The light of the sun shining in from the eastern horizon was reaching the back of the cave. He walked across the smooth ground, entering a wider portion of the cavern, nearly two storeys tall. There before him on the walls were thousands of drawings, from floor to ceiling.

Aldwyn didn't know where to look first. His eyes

darted from one vivid image to the next. He was no scholar, but he could tell these were pieces of Vastia's history recorded in colour. Yet something seemed strange about these cave paintings – tails, paws, hooves – and that's when it hit him: there were no people in the paintings, only animals.

Aldwyn stepped up on a grey boulder to get a closer look at one of the scenes. It was a picture of the Ebs, drawn from the very same spot where, just two days ago, Skylar had told them of the great wizard who had raised the cliffs to turn the river. It was this very act that was being shown here – but the wizard moving mountains was no man. He was – a dog!

Aldwyn moved on to another painting and found another recognisable image, that of the sun being carried across the sky, just like he had seen in the Sun Temple in Bridgetower. The same horse pulled the golden orb behind him, only he was not being ridden by a bearded warrior. The horse was pulling the sun *on his own*.

"Skylar, Gilbert, wake up!" he shouted. "You have to see this!"

Everywhere Aldwyn looked, he saw more

magnificent animal achievements: spiders building a castle, a mouse slaying a dragon, and a pride of cats moving a pillar of granite telekinetically across the plains. All without the help of humans.

Aldwyn was trying to understand what he was seeing. Skylar flew over and sat on the rock beside him. "Is everything OK?" she asked.

But before he was able to respond, Skylar saw the drawings. She fell silent.

"What does it all mean?" asked Aldwyn.

Skylar was still too lost in the discovery to answer. Aldwyn had the sense that what they had stumbled across was profound, deeply meaningful in ways he didn't yet know. Finally, Skylar was able to speak.

"If what I'm seeing on these walls is true, then everything we've ever been told about Vastia's ancient history is a lie. If these paintings aren't the work of a madman, then it was the animals who once were the great wizards of the land, not the humans."

Gilbert hopped over sleepily.

"What's going on?" he asked.

"These are the markings of the Enchantaissance," continued Skylar, pointing from her perch on the rock to a series of symbols drawn beneath the images. Aldwyn recognised them; they were almost identical to the carvings on the Glyphstone in Bridgetower. "The history books state this was a period of magical innovation and artistic wonder for humans. But what if the birds and the beasts first ruled the land? What if before we were the animal companions to wizards and witches, we were the conjurers?"

"I am so lost right now," said Gilbert.

"The paintings," said Aldwyn. "Look."

Gilbert turned to gaze at the hidden history of Vastia. He seemed to have difficulty taking it all in, but then his eyes suddenly lit up.

"Is that a *frog* sitting on that throne?" he asked, dumbfounded.

Reeling a bit, Gilbert stepped back and leaned against the rock on which Aldwyn and Skylar were sitting.

"Why?" asked Skylar, aloud to herself. "Why would history have been rewritten?"

It was just then that Aldwyn spotted something out

of the corner of his eye. He could have sworn that the rock he was sitting on just blinked.

"Umm, guys," he said, but it was too late: again the rock blinked, and then it moved. The grey mass of what he thought was stone was in fact a living creature! A living creature that was now rising to its feet. Aldwyn tried to hold on, but as the cave monster moved upright, his paws lost their grip and he was sent falling to the ground.

Aldwyn crashed to the hard floor and had but a moment to size up the beast now towering at least eight feet above them. Its skin was grey and stony; its chin, nose and ears as sharp as jagged rocks. No wonder Aldwyn had mistaken the creature for a boulder while it had been asleep.

"What is it?" asked Aldwyn.

"A cave troll," answered Gilbert. "And I think we just woke it from its hibernation."

The cave troll stretched its long lumbering arms overhead and yawned, expelling a gust of mildewy breath. It used the backs of its stubby hands to rub the black sleeping crust from its huge eyes. The trio of familiars, cornered in the back of the cavern, knew there was only one way out: through the same opening they had entered the night before. As they began to make a run for it, the troll stomped its foot and let out a grunt, shaking the ground so violently that it knocked Aldwyn and Gilbert off their feet. It scooped up a chunk of rock and hurled it with cannon-like force at the trespassers. Aldwyn dived to one side, Gilbert to the other, and the rock shattered against the wall behind them, sending dust everywhere.

"Over here," called Skylar, who was hiding in a hole in the back wall of the cave. Her fellow familiars darted inside, joining her in the tight, confined space.

The troll reached for them, but its hand was too wide and thick to fit through the hole. Frustrated, the creature pounded its six-fingered fists into the cave wall, trying to break through with sheer force. Its blows sent dust falling from the top of the hole onto the familiars. A pungent sulphurous smell quickly filled the air.

"A volcano must have formed these mountains," said Skylar, wincing from the scent. She reached down and swept some of the residue onto her wing. "This is lava spice."

"Does it kill cave trolls?" asked a trembling Gilbert, as the rocky beast continued to pummel the wall.

"No, but when you mix it with colossus sap—"

"—it can make a person grow up to double their size," Aldwyn completed Skylar's sentence, remembering Kalstaff's lesson from the Forest Under the Trees.

"That's right," said Skylar. "If we all swallow a drop, we can make this a fair fight."

Another mighty punch from the troll cracked the barrier protecting the familiars. It wouldn't be long before their entire defence crumbled.

Skylar reached for her satchel, but it wasn't there!

"My satchel!" she cried, suddenly in a panic. "It must have slipped off while I was flying for the hole."

Aldwyn looked out past the troll, who was still punching furiously, and not far behind it on the floor lay the satchel. It would mean certain death for any of the familiars to try to retrieve it.

"Aldwyn—" Skylar began to say.

"I know, I know," he interrupted. "My telekinesis."

Aldwyn knew his supposed magical talent would be called on again, he just didn't anticipate it would be this soon. He had to confess. He looked down, building up his courage, and there at his feet he saw a fragment of red and silver rock – just like the one that Jack's marbles had been magnetically drawn to.

The troll pounded the cave wall again.

"Aldwyn, hurry up," shouted Skylar. "Use your mind!"

Aldwyn might not have had telekinesis, but he had a different idea. He sneakily picked up the rock in his teeth and leaned his head as far out from the hole as he could towards Skylar's pouch. He just hoped Scribius had enough metal in him for this to work.

Aldwyn thought to himself – *move, move, move.*

The pouch began to shake a little, then slide across the stone floor.

"He's doing it!" said Gilbert excitedly.

Skylar's pouch was moving faster and faster, until it shot through the troll's legs and came to a stop right before Aldwyn's feet. Without the others seeing, he tossed the rock aside.

There was no time for congratulations, but Gilbert was clearly impressed. Skylar quickly removed the vial of colossus sap.

"Gilbert, Aldwyn, add some of that spice to this

vial," she said. "I'll try to distract the troll with an illusion."

Smash!

She dropped the vial into Gilbert's hand just as the troll's thick forearm bashed through the wall, leaving the trio of animals exposed.

"*Nocturno infury!*" chanted Skylar.

Out from the dark, a large woolly bat with giant fangs and breathing fire emerged. Aldwyn would have expected any rational being to duck for cover, but the cave troll didn't seem the least bit intimidated. It swung a fist at the bat, but its hand went straight through the illusion. This sent the troll temporarily off-balance. Aldwyn didn't waste any time, seizing the moment to quickly gather pawfuls of the lava spice and pour them into the glass vial. As the troll stumbled into the wall, Gilbert finished stirring the potion with one of his orange fingers.

He was about to pass Aldwyn the vial when the troll regained its balance and snatched Gilbert up from the ground.

"Oh, boy!" cried Gilbert.

"Drink the potion," shouted Aldwyn.

As the cave dweller lifted the tree frog towards its mouth, Gilbert brought the potion to his lips, but in his panic he dropped the vial directly into the troll's open mouth. Momentarily confused, the monster swallowed and dropped Gilbert back to the ground.

"I'm so sorry," said Gilbert to his companions. "It was an accident!"

Then their enemy started to twitch and expand. First its ears, then its arms and all the way down to its legs, everything was getting bigger, wider and denser. Dim-witted a creature though it was, the cave troll realised that it was growing into an even greater threat and a terrifying smile appeared on its rocky lips. It raised its now elephant-sized foot above Aldwyn and thrust it down, just missing his tail. If the beast's strength had been mighty before, now it was downright awesome.

There was nowhere for the familiars to run. They huddled up shoulder to shoulder in the corner as the enormous troll approached.

"It was an honour fighting by your sides," said Skylar.

"Likewise," replied Gilbert. "And I'm sorry I ever called you an arrogant know-it-all."

"I never heard you say that."

"Well, it wasn't to your face."

The animals braced themselves as the troll clenched its now boulder-sized fist tightly, preparing to crush them. Then there was a loud crack and bits of painted rock started raining down: the troll had grown so large that its head hit the ceiling of the cave. It tried to bend over, but it just kept getting bigger and bigger. Soon it was wedged tightly between the ground and the ceiling, and more and bigger rocks started falling from the crumbling roof of the cave. "Run," shouted Aldwyn to his companions, and they slipped through a sliver of space between the troll's expanding ankles. The walls were spiderwebbing, cracks spreading from every spot the giant was squeezed against. The pictures from the Enchantaissance began to fall away, shattering on the floor below.

"Quick!" screamed Aldwyn. "The whole cave is going to crumble."

Despite Aldwyn's warning, Skylar hesitated, taking a last look at Vastia's forgotten history. She grabbed a painted sliver of cave wall off the ground and slipped it into her pouch. But before she took off, Skylar's silver anklet got pulled to one of the magnetic rocks on the floor. She glanced down, then to Aldwyn. A suspicious look crossed her face.

"Come on!" urged Aldwyn. Skylar gave a tug, pulling her anklet free, and flew for the exit

Then the pressure got too great and the troll's head exploded through the ceiling, straight out into the snowy peaks above. As the familiars darted out of the mouth of the cave, it collapsed, burying the troll's giant body under tons of ancient rock.

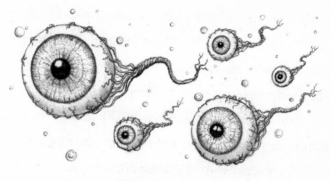

THIRTEEN

The Mountain Alchemist

The familiars had pulled off another narrow escape. As they left the mountain cave behind them, Aldwyn turned back to see the troll's head sticking out from the rubble. It was grunting so loud that the ground shook. Skylar insisted they move fast, as the howling cave troll would most certainly awaken others, sure to be hibernating in nearby caverns. Not that there wasn't a sense of urgency already: the final sunset would be here soon and they hadn't even reached the

Mountain Alchemist, let alone the Sunken Palace.

Once back on the trail and safely away from the cave, Skylar consulted Scribius's map again. "This way," she said after a moment, and Aldwyn thought he detected a new note of self-confidence in the blue jay's voice. It wasn't as if she'd been shy about her skills before, but Aldwyn couldn't help but wonder whether what they had seen in the cave had made his friend even more assured of her importance. He found the notion of this secret animal history intriguing as well, but not having any magic skills himself, their discovery didn't mean as much to him as it did to Skylar.

The trio walked under an overhanging rock outcrop with melting icicles dangling from its ceiling. As they passed beneath it, the thawing crystals dropped water on their heads, giving them an unpleasantly icy shower that washed off the dust of the crumbling cave. Luckily, once they got back into the sun, the warmth of the rays soon dried fur, feathers and skin.

Climbing higher above the clouds, Aldwyn was greeted by a puffy layer of white stretching as far as his eyes could see, like he was staring down at the soft wool coats of a million sheep. Only three peaks pierced through the peaceful cloud cover. It was no wonder that the billy goat had chosen this place for his meditation. Being there made Aldwyn feel a calm he had never experienced before.

Skylar brought them to a stop beside a mountain spring. She pointed her wing to the base of the three peaks.

"So that must be where the Mountain Alchemist resides," she said.

Aldwyn thought it was an appropriate location for a recluse, for finding it had been no small accomplishment.

"Guys, over here," called out Gilbert. "I'm having another viewing."

Aldwyn looked over to see Gilbert staring into the mountain spring.

"It's our loyals," continued Gilbert excitedly.

Aldwyn and Skylar rushed to his side. There in the cool blue waters Aldwyn could see Jack, Marianne and Dalton shackled and exhausted. The glow of Kalstaff's protective forcefields was dimmer now, their strength obviously fading.

"Oh, no," said Gilbert. "It looks like there's some kind of monster behind them. And it's angry."

Aldwyn saw what Gilbert was referring to.

"It's coming into focus now," added Gilbert. "It's got big eyes and fangs. It's opening its mouth. Marianne, look out!"

"Gilbert," Aldwyn said, "I don't think that's part of the viewing." Beneath the surface of the spring, the razor-sharp teeth of a fish-like creature smiled up at Gilbert.

"What do you mean?" asked Gilbert

Just then, the creature launched itself out of the water towards the frog, its teeth narrowly missing his throat. To Gilbert's horror, it landed in the snow and began using its flippers to slide like a seal to pursue him. Gilbert hopped this way and that, but his pursuer was well-suited to manoeuvring on land as well as in the water.

"Do something!" cried Gilbert. "It's going to kill me."

"It's a young piranhadon. It just wants something to eat," said Skylar. "Give it your flies."

Gilbert pulled the flower bud backpack from his

shoulder as he continued to jump just out of the creature's reach. He reluctantly tossed the bud into the piranhadon's mouth, but after swallowing it whole and giving a satisfied burp, the creature simply resumed its chase.

Then Aldwyn had an idea. He stuck his paw into Jack's pouch and began rummaging, past the remaining clovers, past the glow-worm... there it was! He removed the piece of white toffee, took aim – and threw it straight into the creature's gaping mouth. When the piranhadon chomped down next, its teeth got stuck together. The creature stopped its pursuit of Gilbert and became increasingly angry as it tried to open its mouth. No longer able to attack, it slid back to the mountain spring and disappeared into the water.

Gilbert, out of breath, hugged Aldwyn with gratitude. "You saved me!" he croaked. "And you," turning to Skylar, "made me sacrifice my flies for nothing!"

"That was certainly unusual," said Skylar, ignoring him. "Piranhadons don't typically inhabit such high altitudes. We're fortunate there wasn't an entire school of them."

"You owe me a flower bud of flies," said Gilbert, still angry with her.

Skylar continued to ignore him. A moment later she was hit by a massive snowball! Her beak and body got wedged into the dense powder, and Aldwyn and Gilbert could only watch with horror as she was swept down the mountain by the growing ball of snow. It picked up speed and snow as Skylar disappeared inside it. Then Aldwyn saw where the snowball was headed: straight towards the edge of the mountain.

"Skylar!" cried Gilbert.

And then the unthinkable happened: the mass of snow rolled off the mountainside, with Skylar still trapped within it. Aldwyn and Gilbert just stood there, shell-shocked.

They were still staring – to Aldwyn it felt like an eternity – when Skylar flew up from beyond the edge of the mountain, shaking flakes of white from her feathers. Aldwyn and Gilbert ran towards her.

"You're OK!" said Gilbert, hugging her awkwardly.

"You gave us a real scare," said Aldwyn.

"Well, it's a good thing I know how to fly. Neither of you would have been so lucky."

After continuing up the hill, the familiars discovered what was responsible for the attack: a hand made of snow, packing more snowballs for whoever might attempt to ascend the peak next. Skylar said, "It's some kind of permanent protective spell. Looks like the Mountain Alchemist isn't too keen on visitors."

"I know you said he wanted to be alone," said Aldwyn. "But don't you think trying to *kill* your visitors is going too far?"

"The piranhadon must have been his doing as well," added Skylar, as the trio skirted around the hand and trekked further on, now constantly on the lookout for the next threat. Threats that would keep them from getting the precious powder needed to put the seven-headed hydra to sleep.

Eventually, they arrived at the base of the three peaks, where they spotted a quaint wooden cottage on the far side of a frozen lake. Through the window, they could see the flickering light of a fire, where Aldwyn imagined the alchemist was warming his toes.

"When we get there, let me do the talking," Skylar reminded the others as they set off across the frozen water. "It may take some persuasion to convince him to help us. But that sleeping powder is our only hope of saving Dalton, Marianne and—"

Clunk!

Skylar's statement was cut short as she flew headfirst into an invisible wall and slid down its surface back onto the ice. Aldwyn stretched out his paw in front of him and felt something as smooth and hard as steel blocking their path.

"He must have cast a *porticul*," said Skylar, still rubbing her head. "It's a forcefield. A final barrier to keep out visitors."

Skylar flew high but could find no top or hole in the wall.

"It's solid," she said, when she had landed next to Aldwyn and Gilbert again. "And it could take us days to find an opening in it."

"I bet Marianne would have been able to conjure a telegate to get us through," said Gilbert.

"Well, I could have, too," replied Skylar, sounding slightly miffed. "But all my proper components were destroyed by the fire in Kalstaff's cottage."

While they argued, Aldwyn's attention was drawn below the ice, where a school of minnows were swimming. They circled beneath his paws and then darted off in the direction of the cabin. It didn't register at first, but after a second moment of thought, it appeared that there wasn't a forcefield underwater. The fish were gliding freely back and forth between them and the cottage. Perhaps Aldwyn could use the same trick he pulled off when a tall stone wall was built around Bridgetower's dairy house: if you couldn't climb over something, try going *under* it.

"So what do we do now?" asked Gilbert.

"You're the one who can see into the future," replied Skylar. "You tell me."

"Guys," said Aldwyn, but neither of them stopped to listen.

"You know my puddle viewings don't work that way," said Gilbert.

"That's because they don't work at all!"

They continued arguing, so Aldwyn decided to test out his theory on his own. While there were few things less appealing to a cat than a dip in freezing cold water, all Aldwyn had to do to get himself moving was remind himself of one thing: Jack. He stretched out his claws and cut a circle around himself in the ice.

Beneath his weight, the ice gave way, sending him sinking into the freezing water.

Within a moment, Aldwyn was completely underwater. Only the dense, heavy sound of water rushing up against ice filled his ears. A shock of cold hit his system, but he paddled through the chalky blue, holding his breath tightly in his lungs. He only travelled a tiny distance, just far enough to move past the forcefield, before he started clawing at the frozen ceiling above him, creating a hole for escape.

After a frantic scrabble through the ice Aldwyn shot his head up through the opening, breathing in as he pulled himself back to the surface. On the other side, Skylar and Gilbert were still quarrelling, unaware of what Aldwyn had been up to. He used the back of his paw to knock on the invisible wall. Skylar and Gilbert turned and did a double take.

Aldwyn saw Gilbert's lips move through the soundproof barricade and it looked like he was saying Aldwyn's name. Aldwyn began pointing at the hole in the ice on their side, then to the one on his.

"Through there," he said.

Skylar and Gilbert exchanged some words. Aldwyn

wasn't exactly sure what they were talking about, but it appeared Skylar was nervous and Gilbert was giving her some encouragement. He took the plunge first, then Skylar held her breath and flew beneath the surface as well. Aldwyn waited. And waited. Their underwater passage was taking longer than his own. He was starting to wonder if something had gone wrong. Then Skylar surfaced, pushed up through the hole by Gilbert, who was right below her. Aldwyn helped them both out of the icy lake. Skylar shivered, coughing up water.

"Thanks," she said to Gilbert

The tree frog smiled. Aldwyn knew Gilbert didn't receive a lot of compliments from Skylar.

"And good thinking," the blue jay added, giving Aldwyn his due as well. "Now let's get to the cottage."

The trio didn't have far to go. They reached the end of the lake quickly and made their final approach to the alchemist's cabin. The dwelling looked to be about the same size as Kalstaff's. Icicles dangled from the snow-covered rooftop.

Aldwyn and Gilbert were about to step onto the porch leading to the front door when Skylar cried

"Wait!" They froze in their tracks. "Don't move."

Aldwyn and Gilbert looked at her quizzically. Had the icy water done something to Skylar's brain?

"This cottage is an illusion," she said. "Look at the icicles."

Aldwyn glanced up. They appeared real enough to him.

"The sun has been out for hours," she explained. "They should be melting, but there's not a drop of water coming from them."

Aldwyn realised that Skylar was right: in spite of being exposed to full sunlight, the icicles were completely frozen. Skylar swooped down and picked up a stone, then flung it at the cottage's front window. The rock passed right through the illusion. The cottage evaporated and Aldwyn could see what was actually before him: nothing. The Mountain Alchemist had set one final trap. Any unsuspecting travellers who stepped onto his illusion of a porch would have found themselves falling down a sheer cliff.

"His actual cottage won't be too far from here," said Skylar. "Even a powerful illusionist needs to stay close to maintain a creation as large as this."

And indeed, once the familiars had rounded a cluster of rocks, they saw an identical-looking cabin – and this time the icicles hanging from the roof were dripping. Still, Aldwyn advanced cautiously, but Skylar went right up to the front door and knocked on it with her beak.

The door swung open and the three animals entered, finding themselves in a sitting room that doubled as a kitchen. It was sparsely furnished, with only a plain wooden table and a single chair in its centre. A small pot sat on the fire, cooking what smelled like a very bland meal. Down the hall, the trio saw another lighted room, and they quietly moved towards it.

They peeked through the crack in the door, and there was the Mountain Alchemist, sitting in a rocking chair. His eyes seemed normal save for the pupils, which were a milky white. His skin was tanned from snowburn. While Aldwyn knew the alchemist was about as old as Kalstaff and Queen Loranella, his wrinkles and hunched appearance made him seem much older. His fingertips were stained all different colours, no doubt by the chemicals and other ingredients he had used to concoct magic potions and spells. In this room filled with empty bookshelves, there was only one book, and it rested in his lap. The alchemist's finger was passing over the page. Although the words written there were not raised or marked for the unseeing, it was as if he could understand the text just by touching the patterns of ink swirling across the parchment.

"One good book is all you need," said the old wizard, "once you've read them all."

The familiars just stood there, not sure how to respond.

"Now identify yourselves, before I turn you all into dust. There is no language that I do not understand, including animal tongue."

Skylar cleared her throat.

"We apologise for intruding," she said. "I am Skylar. My companions are Aldwyn and Gilbert. We come from Stone Runlet."

"What do you want? A youth potion? Something that can turn metal into gold? Whatever it is, you've risked your lives for nothing."

"Please," said Skylar. "Kalstaff was our teacher."

"Kalstaff?" said the Mountain Alchemist, surprised. "That's a name I haven't heard in a long time. Continue."

"He's dead," said Skylar.

The alchemist paused. For the first time, his unsmiling face softened. But only for a moment.

"What happened?"

"Queen Loranella killed him."

He leaned forwards in his chair.

"That can't be."

"We were there," said Skylar. "We saw it. And she kidnapped our loyals. Kalstaff says they are the prophesised three."

"So it begins again," said the alchemist. He sat for a long time thinking, then spoke once more. "Sixty years ago, Vastia was threatened by a great evil, the dark mages Wyvern and Skull. They raised the Dead Army and tried to conquer all the land. But a prophecy in the sky told of three young spellcasters who were destined to defeat them. I was one, Kalstaff and Loranella the others. Together, along with the Royal Guard, we fought back the army and restored peace to the queendom."

The familiars remained silent.

"At the end of the decisive battle, Loranella delivered the deadly blow that ended the war. She was judged the noblest and most pure of heart among us, and was crowned queen of Vastia. Kalstaff became her most trusted adviser and protector. I declined a life in the palace, instead settling here for quiet study, in search of answers to puzzles and the mysteries of the Tomorrowlife. Long have I been removed from matters of the queendom, but never could I have guessed that such wickedness would enter Loranella's heart."

"We don't yet know what end she seeks," said Skylar. "But it is clear that our loyals are the key to stopping her. A puddle viewing revealed that they are being held captive in the Sunken Palace."

"That explains why you're here," replied the alchemist. "You've come to ask me for my sleeping powder."

Skylar was taken aback. "How did you know?"

"Because I've used it once before. Loranella, Kalstaff and I ventured inside those old palace walls during the Uprising, seeking a wooden bracelet secured in the throne room. But before we could cross the main hall, we were confronted by the Hydra of Mukrete. It was my powder that put it to sleep, but not before the smallest and most vicious of the heads spat acid in my eyes, blinding me permanently. Not even the magical ravens could heal the damage."

The alchemist fell silent, caught up in the memories of heroic deeds long past. Then he rose to his feet, placing the book on his chair. "Follow me," he said. Without a cane or even the aid of the wall, he led the familiars towards another room at the back of the cottage.

"He gets around pretty well for a blind guy," whispered Aldwyn to Skylar.

"Yes, my senses are highly trained," replied the alchemist, who blocked Gilbert's tongue as it shot out to snag a lone moth fluttering overhead.

They walked into a wide, open room, with large glass windows looking out over the clouds. The snow had begun to fall once more, but this time in light flurries. A large apothecary's chest stood against the far wall. Hundreds of tiny drawers, each with worn knobs and chipped paint, looked as if they had been opened and closed a thousand times. The alchemist picked up a single beaker that was suspended a foot off the ground by a metal vice. The only other thing present in the room was a giant tortoiseshell sitting beneath the windows.

"Edan, wake up," said the alchemist. But the tortoise didn't budge. The alchemist walked over and used his knuckle to tap on the outside of Edan's shell. "Anybody home?"

A tan-coloured head slowly poked out from beneath the tortoiseshell, along with the turtle's front and hind legs. Aldwyn now remembered seeing the very same turtle in the picture on Kalstaff's table. So this was the alchemist's familiar, the one who had been at his side during the Dead Army Uprising. Aldwyn couldn't help but wonder what use this slow moving reptile would be in the heat of battle.

The alchemist had moved to the apothecary's chest. He put his hand on the top left corner of the cabinet and slid his fingers quickly down the side, feeling the bumps in the texture of the wood. When he reached two-thirds of the way down, he began dragging his fingers horizontally across the knobs, mumbling to himself as he did so. Once he got about half way, he pulled open the drawer and removed what appeared to be freshly picked golden flowers. He crushed them in his hand and let the pieces fall into the beaker.

His fingers were moving again, in the same way as before, following a system he had clearly perfected. With incredible speed and confidence, the alchemist found three more components, and added each one to the glass tube.

"Now we just cook it for the length of an entire day," said the alchemist as he returned the beaker to the metal vice.

"A whole day?" asked Aldwyn.

"We can't wait that long," said Gilbert.

"Kalstaff put a protective spell over our loyals," explained Skylar, "but it will fade by sundown tonight."

"Oh, quiet down, all of you," said the alchemist. "I have awakened Edan for just that."

The alchemist snapped his fingers and a fire materialised below the beaker, beginning to heat the ingredients mixed inside it. Edan closed his eyes and lowered his head to the ground. A translucent shell formed around the beaker, the Mountain Alchemist, the familiars and the giant tortoise.

Aldwyn looked around. He wasn't exactly sure what was happening, but it seemed as if outside the shell, time had stopped. The snowflakes outside the window hung in midair. The moth, too, was motionless in mid-flight, its wings still.

"How did——"Aldwyn started to ask, but he was cut off.

"Edan is one of the last remaining time stoppers," said the alchemist. "Within this shell, time will move at its own pace, while outside of it, nary a moment shall pass until the shell is removed. Whether time passes faster in the bubble or the world outside it slows down is a puzzle for great thinkers – a true philosopher's dilemma. Either way, for us, a whole day will go by; for that moth, it'll be less than one beat of its wings."

"Is that why you look so much older than Kalstaff?" asked Gilbert. "Because you've been living in a bubble – I mean, a shell?"

"Gilbert!" scolded Skylar.

"I can see Kalstaff has taught you little in the way of manners. But yes, I have spent many an extra decade within Edan's shells. And while it has aged me, it has also given me time to learn so much more."

The alchemist began stirring the beaker with a slender metal rod.

"Take this opportunity to rest, familiars," said Edan in a quiet, even-tempered voice, speaking for the first time. "I know how trying this quest must be for you."

Aldwyn didn't need to be told twice. A nap in complete safety sounded like a wonderful idea. He curled up on the floor, closed his eyes and within seconds was fast asleep.

FOURTEEN

An Unwelcome Return

When Aldwyn woke from the most peaceful sleep of his life, the Mountain Alchemist was carefully corking a small vial filled with a yellow-coloured powder. Skylar and Gilbert were already awake and looked as if they had been busy occupying themselves for some time. Skylar had just finished organising the contents of her satchel. Gilbert was looking out at the moth, a tasty treat just out of tongue and time's reach.

"It's ready," said the alchemist, "and it's as strong as anything I have ever brewed."

He held out his palm with the vial resting atop it.

"Here, take it," he said. "The only way to put the beast to sleep is by throwing a pinch of the powder into its eyes."

Skylar flew over and took the glass tube in her claws.

"Which of the seven heads should we use it on?" she asked.

"All of them."

Why did that not surprise Aldwyn? It seemed every challenge the familiars had faced since the young wizards had been kidnapped was more difficult than it first appeared.

"The powder affects the brain, not the body," continued the alchemist. "And the hydra has seven brains. Each must be put to sleep for you to have a chance of passage."

"Good thing we've got Aldwyn's telekinesis," said Gilbert.

"Uh, well, you know, that sounds like it requires some pin-point accuracy," Aldwyn stuttered. "Which of course I am capable of, but it may be better to let Skylar fly the powder into the hydra's eyes."

The blue jay carried the vial over to Aldwyn and passed it to him.

"I think it will be a lot safer for all of us if you use your telekinesis," she said. Aldwyn reluctantly slipped it into Jack's pouch.

"Edan," said the alchemist, "let's rejoin the normal flow of time once more."

The giant tortoise lifted his head from the ground and the shell surrounding them disappeared. The snow outside started to fall again and the moth's wings fluttered once more, as if they had never stopped.

"You should know that I only assisted you because I owed Kalstaff for a wrong I committed against him long ago," said the alchemist. "But now that wrong has been righted, so don't return asking for my help again."

He turned his back on the familiars and walked over to the two large windows through which he could not see. Aldwyn looked at him curiously. What betrayal did this great magician commit against Kalstaff? What would weigh so heavily on his conscience all these years later?

"Thank you," Skylar called back to Edan as she headed for the door.

"Forgive him for his gruffness," replied the turtle, "and know that I do not share his intolerance. It is toughness and talent we have in common, not temperament. Good luck."

The three familiars hurried down the hall and out through the front door into the bitter cold outside, ready for the final, most dangerous part of their adventure. From this point they would be heading east towards the sandy plateaux below, following the path Skylar plotted for them along Scribius's map. They hiked a trail around the base of the trident peak. There on its far side they saw another cottage identical in appearance to the alchemist's, no doubt an illusion set to trap unwelcome visitors coming up the other side. Aldwyn felt sorry for any traveller who wasn't accompanied by someone with Skylar's keen eye for observation.

The trip down the mountain was far less strenuous than the one up. Gravity did most of the work. Aldwyn's paws were just becoming accustomed to the constant chill of the snow and ice when the terrain began to change. Over the next few hours, the slope flattened into a long stretch of elevated plains and the temperature rose with every step. Now warm grains of sand were getting stuck between Aldwyn's toes.

Soon, the trio was baking in the valley heat. A lone tree here, a dried shrub there, and the occasional stone arch – nothing else offered the animals refuge from the beating sun. Aldwyn could only imagine how hot it would be here if Vastia wasn't experiencing unseasonably cold weather. Gilbert began to slow under the harsh desert-like conditions. The only relief came when the tree frog moistened his forehead with his own tongue. He continued to plod along behind Aldwyn and Skylar, asking every five minutes if they were there yet, until finally a vision appeared before them.

"Please don't be a mirage," said Gilbert.

As they got closer, Aldwyn saw it, too: a thin band of water flowing through a crack in the ground.

"No, it's real," said Aldwyn.

Gilbert forgot his exhaustion and charged for the cool stream. By the time Aldwyn and Skylar got there Gilbert was neck deep in the water.

"Come on in," he called. "It feels great. And no piranhadons!"

Aldwyn decided to just splash a few drops on his fur; Skylar passed altogether.

"I thought you would have been more excited to be here," said Skylar to Aldwyn.

"Sure, the water's pleasant, but I don't really mind the heat."

"I was talking about here, on the plateau," she said.

Aldwyn looked at her, not sure what she was talking about.

"In Maidenmere," she said. "Your home."

"Oh, well, yes," he said quickly, trying to cover up his initial confusion. "Of course I'm excited about that. It's always nice to be back on the old stamping grounds. I love this place. Some of my best memories."

Aldwyn could see that Skylar was looking at him sceptically, the same way she had after the chameleon crab and cave troll incidents.

"Hey, Gilbert, you almost finished in there?" asked Aldwyn, eager to get moving. "Now's really not the time for a soak."

Gilbert dunked his head under one last time.

"I feel completely refreshed," said the tree frog, hopping out of the stream and onto a smooth neighbouring rock. That's when Aldwyn and Skylar both saw that Gilbert was covered in winged leeches, their fangs embedded into his skin.

"Um, Gilbert—" said Skylar, pointing at him with her wing.

"I am ready to go," said Gilbert, still oblivious to the bloodsuckers pulsating all over his body. "I'm telling you, you two really missed out. You should have joined me."

He took a couple of jumps towards them, then looked down. There was a moment of shock, followed by screaming.

"Ahhhhhhhh!" he shrieked. "Vampire leeches! They're going to drain me of all my blood."

"Relax," said Skylar. "We'll get them off."

"How?" asked Gilbert in a panic.

"Luckily, we're in Aldwyn's home," said Skylar. "We'll just ask his pride for help."

Aldwyn did a double take. This was very bad.

"You know, leech removing really isn't my people's

speciality," he said, fully aware that he sounded rather desperate. "I'm sure they'll just fall off on their own when they've had their fill."

"Each of these suckers can drink a jug of blood," said Skylar. "By the time they've had their fill, Gilbert will be dead. We need a clove of garlic, and we need it right now."

Before the words even left her mouth, Skylar took to the air, leaving Aldwyn little choice but to chase after her. A dizzy and weakening Gilbert hobbled beside him.

"Gilbert's looking better already," Aldwyn called up to Skylar, hoping to change her mind.

But there was no question that the tree frog was in fact becoming worse. He had turned from his healthy green to a pale yellow and his eyes were starting to roll back in his head.

"Ooooh, stars," he babbled.

"Stay with me, Gilbert," said Aldwyn.

"Over here, over here!" Skylar called out to some figures beyond the trees.

Aldwyn could see that she was beckoning two bicoloured cats. They really did look remarkably like him, so no wonder he had been mistaken by everybody for one of their kind. But somehow he knew that he wouldn't be able to fool an actual cat from Maidenmere about his humble, magicless origins.

The two cats approached. When they spotted the leech-covered Gilbert, they immediately signalled to the familiars to follow them.

"Aldwyn," said Gilbert woozily. "I see three of you."

He collapsed, hitting the ground with a thud.

"Put him on my back," said the bigger of the two Maidenmere cats.

Aldwyn and Skylar hoisted their lightheaded friend onto the cat. Gilbert dangled limply as they all began a hurried walk towards a group of unusual rock formations too far in the distance to make out clearly.

"Aldwyn here is one of you," said Skylar, hoping to win as much favour as she could, given their desperate situation.

"Yes, a fellow cat, we can see that," said the one bearing Gilbert.

"No, he is from Maidenmere, as well," she added.

"Is that so?" asked the other, the white-chinned one. "I'm a Stream Chaser. Kafar comes from the Whistling Rock. What family were you born to?"

"Desert Cactus," replied Aldwyn, eyeing a... desert cactus.

The two cats exchanged a look.

"Never heard of it," said the one called Kafar. "But there are so many it's difficult to keep track."

Aldwyn was readying himself for the next question, but none came. As the group hurried across the plateau, Aldwyn got a closer look at the unusual rock formations he had seen from a distance. They were actually floating above the ground! It was a breathtaking sight. Islands of rock were levitating a small tree's height above the ground. Each had stairs that led up to them, or more accurately, a series of free-floating stones arranged like stairs and held telekinetically in the air.

All around them, on each floating island, black-and-white cats could be seen, looking down at the strangers below with a certain amount of curiosity and suspicion. Many more walked the ground beneath.

"There should be garlic stored in the community

cave," said Kafar. "It's just up ahead."

Gilbert was still breathing and the vampire leeches were still sucking, growing larger with every swallow of the tree frog's blood.

"We're almost there," said Skylar, comforting him.

As they continued, Aldwyn saw a litter of kittens practising beginner's telekinesis under the guidance of an older cat. Each of the small felines held a leaf stationary in front of their eyes, using only their concentration.

"Now move it in circles," instructed the teacher.

At once, all of the leaves began to dance in unison, spinning round in the air.

Somewhere else, Aldwyn spied a cat sitting before a pile of tinder. Above it, two rough stones were being smashed together, but not by the cat's paws. They seemed to move on their own. A spark shot out from between them, lighting the wood.

Further up ahead, two young cats stood apart motionlessly fencing with sticks controlled only through thought. Neither moved as the weapons clashed, splinters of wood breaking off from the force of the blows. Aldwyn found these feats of telekinesis extraordinary, but he couldn't show it. If he revealed even the slightest bit of wonder, his cover would surely be blown.

The familiars and their two guides reached the cave and entered it. An older female cat was curled up on the ground inside. She stood upon seeing them.

"Please, help our friend," said Skylar. "We need garlic."

"Rest him on the ground," replied the den matron. Gilbert moaned as Kafar lowered him down.

Aldwyn noticed that boxes were already moving further back in the cave, rearranging themselves as if to make way for something. Out from below, a small chest rose up and swung open its lid. A bulb of garlic was telekinetically pulled out and carried over towards Gilbert. In midair it broke into six cloves. Each was guided to a cluster of leeches. The garlic wedges rubbed furiously against the slimy backs of the vampire bloodsuckers, causing them to detach from Gilbert with a screech. They flapped their black leathery wings and darted for the mouth of the cave, leaving a trail of Gilbert's blood dripping from their fangs as they flew off.

When Aldwyn looked up again, a clay pot was rising through the air. Once it reached Gilbert, it tipped gently, pouring a clear salve on the bite marks that were covering his body. As the ointment dissolved into the open wounds, it began to fizz and bubble, healing them quickly. Gilbert sat up with a start, gasping for air.

"Easy," said the old cat. "It would be wise to rest for a while."

"Unfortunately, we don't have time for that," said Aldwyn. "In fact, we really must be going."

"You've been a great help," said Skylar. "But he's right. We have a most urgent matter to attend to before today's sunset. I hope one day we can return to properly repay you."

The familiars were escorted outside by Kafar. They didn't get very far, though, before they were approached by a cat with black and white stripes that made him look like a white tiger. Surrounded by a dozen cats, male and female, he had a metal spike through the side of his ear and braids in his tail. A palm leaf floated above his head as he walked, shading him from the sun.

"What do we have here?" asked the charismatic cat, with a purr that couldn't help but draw you closer. "I'd like to know who's trespassing on my land."

"Oh, no, we're not trespassing," said Skylar.

"Well, I didn't invite you," replied the cat, beginning to circle them.

"You misunderstand, Lord Malvern," said Kafar timidly. "This cat is one of us."

"My apologies," said Malvern, but somehow it came out sounding more like a threat. He stared Aldwyn dead in the eyes. "So you are from Maidenmere?"

Aldwyn felt his heart begin to pound in his chest.

"That's right," he stammered. "I was born to the Desert Cactus family."

"Really," said Malvern, with what seemed like the utmost sincerity. "It's so good to have you back, brother. Show us your sand sign."

All eyes were on Aldwyn.

"My sand sign?" asked Aldwyn. He swallowed hard.

"Yes. Do you need a demonstration?" replied Malvern.

From the ground, thousands of grains of sand lifted into the air, forming an elaborate picture of a paw reaching out for the moon.

"The sign of the Mooncatchers," said Malvern, his tone becoming a little more severe.

He let the sands drop back to earth.

"Well?" he said. "What are you waiting for?"

And that's when Aldwyn knew that he wouldn't be able to bluff his way out of this one. He had reached the end of his lie. Skylar and Gilbert looked at him expectantly, but Aldwyn didn't even try to lift the sands. There was simply no point. He was not a cat from Maidenmere. He did not possess telekinetic powers. He had no business impersonating a familiar. He was just an orphaned street cat.

"I can't," said Aldwyn quietly.

"What was that?" asked Malvern. "I didn't hear you."

"I can't do it."

"Come on," encouraged Gilbert. "It doesn't have to be perfect."

"He's probably just nervous," said Skylar, but there was a twinge of doubt in her voice now.

"No, I really can't do it," said Aldwyn. "I'm not who you think I am."

"Indeed you're not. You're a liar," said Malvern. "There's no such family as the Desert Cactus. You're not part of this pride. How dare you pretend to be?"

"What?" asked Gilbert, still sure this was a big misunderstanding. "You can do telekinesis. I've seen it, with my own eyes. Twice."

"No, Gilbert," said Aldwyn. "In Daku, it was chameleon crabs who lifted that branch, not me."

"But Skylar's pouch in the cave. You made it slide to her."

"No, I didn't. It was a magnetic rock. I used it to pull Scribius and the pouch towards me."

The tree frog looked devastated. "And your telepathy?" he asked.

Malvern laughed. "Oh, you can read minds, too? What a talented cat you must be."

Aldwyn felt the mocking eyes of the Maidenmere cats on him.

Skylar was less surprised, but still shaking her head. "I don't understand," she said. "Why?"

There was nothing Aldwyn could say. He just lowered his head.

"Well then," said Malvern. "I think we're finished

here. You'll be escorted from Maidenmere at once."

"Please," said Skylar, turning to Malvern. "I know there's an easy path off the plateau. If you'd just allow us to pass through your land, we'll be gone quickly."

"We welcomed you here, saved your friend. And in return, you lied to us." Malvern's eyes narrowed. "Impostors are not welcome in our home. You'll have to cross over the Torentia Falls and make a trail down the other side."

"We don't have time for that," pleaded Skylar. "Our loyals have been—"

"Enough," said Malvern coldly, cutting her off. "Your problems are not mine."

Malvern turned and walked to one of the large, floating islands. He climbed the levitating stone stairway and disappeared among the rocks.

A group of bicolours surrounded the familiars and led them out of the village. Aldwyn couldn't look Skylar and Gilbert in the eye. He wanted to apologise, make things right, tell them this wasn't at all what he had intended. But saying the words in his head was different from actually speaking them, and every time he tried his throat seemed to close up on him.

They were left at the stream where Gilbert had made the unfortunate acquaintance of the vampire leeches. Unfortunate in more ways than one, thought Aldwyn sadly.

"If you again set foot on our land, you will be punished," said Kafar before turning away.

The three animals stood there.

"Give us the sleeping powder," said Skylar coldly to Aldwyn. "Gilbert and I will continue to the Sunken Palace without you."

Aldwyn shook his head, thinking of Jack in trouble. "No. I want to come."

"Just hand it over," said Skylar furiously. "This is no longer your quest. You never should have been here in the first place."

Aldwyn lowered his head and slid Jack's pouch off his shoulder. He pushed it over to Gilbert, who slung it across his back without saying a word.

"I'm still Jack's familiar, though, aren't I?" asked Aldwyn.

"I don't know what you are any more," said Skylar. "Let's go, Gilbert."

"Wait," Aldwyn called out. "Just because I lied to you about who I was doesn't change how I feel. Jack is the only family I've ever known, and the two of you are my only friends."

"I thought we were a team," said Gilbert sadly.

"We are. Just because I'm not magical doesn't mean I can't help."

"Well, if you'd have just been honest from the beginning, we wouldn't be having this conversation, now would we?" asked Skylar.

"You're the one to talk," said Aldwyn. "I'm not the only one with secrets around here."

"What's that supposed to mean?" she asked.

"Wyvern and Skull's *Tome of the Occult*. You took it from Kalstaff's library."

"That's ridiculous," said Gilbert, quickly coming to Skylar's defence.

"I saw her," said Aldwyn. "She made a pile of bones come to life, using a spell straight out of that book."

"That was different," said Skylar. "And none of your business."

"What?" exclaimed Gilbert. "It was you! Who are you? I feel like I don't know you at all any more."

"And I know you're hiding something about that anklet," continued Aldwyn. "You're not so perfect. Don't stand there and judge me."

"To be the best familiar, it's important to understand all aspects of magic," said Skylar. "Including the darker ones." She paused and thought for a moment. "But you're right. I lied too."

"So we're in agreement," said Aldwyn.

"But one has nothing to do with the other," she replied. "Unlike you, my lies don't make me completely unqualified to be on this journey."

Aldwyn shook his head. "I don't know how many more ways I can say it. I'm sorry. I messed up."

Skylar considered long and hard. Then she gave in and said: "You can follow us across the Falls and down whatever trail we find there. But when we reach the road to the Sunken Palace, we go our separate ways."

She began to fly off, with Gilbert hopping along after her, holding Jack's pouch over his shoulder. Aldwyn followed a few paces behind them. He knew he wouldn't be forgiven easily, but at least it was a start.

FIFTEEN

Torentia Falls

"So, is your name even Aldwyn?" asked Gilbert.

"Of course it is," he answered, glad that somebody was talking to him.

It was late afternoon on the third day of their quest, and the familiars were now trekking northwards towards the Torentia Falls, a slippery, treacherous and, worst of all, time-consuming detour – one that Aldwyn felt more than a little guilty about.

"If you're not from Maidenmere, where are you

from?" continued Gilbert.

"I'm an alley cat from Bridgetower."

"Well, should we be forced to rummage through garbage, you'll be the first we ask for help," said Skylar, acknowledging him for the first time since they'd left Maidenmere.

"OK, I deserved that," Aldwyn said. "But my lowly upbringing has got us out of quite a bit of trouble on this journey."

"We would have been just fine without you," replied Skylar, holding her beak high stubbornly.

"Really? Who thought of hitching that ride on the horse cart? Or throwing the three-leafed clover in the octopot? Or getting us past the Mountain Alchemist's invisible wall?"

"But none of that changes the fact you're not a familiar," said Skylar simply. "You can't do anything magical."

"I can make fish disappear," said Aldwyn, trying to lighten the mood.

Gilbert giggled, unable to stay angry with his friend. That didn't seem to be a problem for Skylar, though.

"Well, the good news is it won't be difficult for you to find your way back home," said Skylar.

"Why's that?" asked Aldwyn.

"Because this is the Ebs," she said, gesturing to the top of the waterfall. "It loops all the way back around the Peaks of Kailasa, straight past the Turn and down to the walls of Bridgetower."

It looked as if Aldwyn would not be changing Skylar's mind after all: she and Gilbert would be continuing on to the Sunken Palace, while he would be setting off in the opposite direction on his own. Perhaps he would return to Bridgetower to scavenge the streets he knew so well, or maybe he'd explore a new city along the way, one where food might be easier to come by. Tammy would probably welcome him for as long as he cared to stay at the inn. But then he thought of Jack and his tail curled involuntarily, the same way it did the very first time his loyal touched him. The boy's life was still in danger, and Aldwyn knew that there was no way he would be able to go back to his old life. He had promised to take care of Jack, and he would be true to his promise, magic or no magic

While Aldwyn was thinking about the best way to talk Skylar into letting him continue on with them, the animals had come to the rocky bank of the rapids. A series of slick boulders and fallen trees made a path to the other side. Further down the river, they could hear the sound of the Ebs River rushing over the edge of the falls and crashing to the unseen rocks below.

"We're lucky the rains have been so light," said Skylar. "Otherwise this would not have been crossable."

She flew ahead as Gilbert and Aldwyn hopped from stone to bark. Splashes of cold water landed on Aldwyn's fur. The crossing would have been smooth if Gilbert had only looked down to see the small patch of algae covering his stepping stone. Unfortunately his eyes were already measuring the distance to the next rock and his foot slipped. As Gilbert's belly hit the stone, Jack's pouch jostled around his neck, flipping upside down, which wouldn't have been a problem had it not been for the hole Agdaleen had punctured through its top with the fire poker. Aldwyn watched as the vial of sleeping powder slid through the opening. The glass tube bounced off the rock before plunking into the water.

"Gilbert, the sleeping powder!" shouted Aldwyn over the sound of the fast-flowing water.

Skylar heard Aldwyn and caught sight of the vial as it drifted rapidly downstream.

Aldwyn began jumping from rock to rock, attempting to catch up with it. Skylar swooped low, but the bobbing vial remained just out of her reach. Gilbert was back on all fours and frantically chasing the powder in order to make up for his clumsiness.

"It's moving too fast," shouted Skylar, swooping down again and again as the vial gathered speed and headed straight for the falls. The water was roaring now, white with foam, and it was almost impossible to keep track of the precious container. Aldwyn had leaped down the river all the way to the last slippery rock before the falls. He was just a few tail lengths away from the giant drop. Then he saw the vial.

"I see it!" he exclaimed. "I think I can catch it." He stretched out his paw to snag the glass tube, but it proved as difficult as fishing an ant out of a bowl of milk. It was at moments like this that he wished he had fingers and thumbs. The vial bounced off his paw, briefly slowed, changed direction, drifted on – and was caught by the branch of a drooping tree.

"Oh, thank goodness," cried Skylar. She soared down and Aldwyn watched her land on the branch. But before she could bend over and grip the vial with her beak, the wood snapped, sending Skylar splashing into the water. Aldwyn reached out to grab the blue jay, but it was too late: both Skylar and the vial went tumbling over the falls. In a last-ditch attempt to help Skylar, Aldwyn reached too far, his hind legs slipped and he went sliding towards the churning waters. Gilbert tried to catch him before he fell, but instead went tumbling in with Aldwyn. Both were swept over the edge of the waterfall.

Aldwyn was spinning through the air in free fall, seeing the mist below and Gilbert just above him. He seemed to fall for an eternity before he hit the water hard and went deep into the plunge pool. When his head came up from the water, he could see a limp Skylar bobbing slowly downstream. Gilbert surfaced just a moment after Aldwyn did.

"The vial!" exclaimed Gilbert as if it were a miracle. "I see it."

"I'm going to get Skylar," said Aldwyn over the roar of the water behind them. "You go after the sleeping powder."

Aldwyn paddled towards Skylar, who was struggling to keep her head from going under once more. When he got close enough, Aldwyn reached out and clamped down on her neck with his mouth, firm enough to get a good grip, but gentle enough so as not to hurt her. With Skylar held between his teeth, Aldwyn let himself drift against the shore, where he dragged her onto dry land.

"Skylar, are you OK?" he asked.

She coughed up some water.

"Where's Gilbert?" she asked. "What happened to the sleeping powder?"

"I got it. It's right here," wheezed Gilbert, hopping to their side and collapsing to the ground, completely out of breath.

Skylar winced in pain as she sat up. "Ow, my wing. I think it's broken."

"Try not to move it," said Aldwyn.

"This is terrible," she said. "I won't be able to fly, and since you lied about your magical talent, we'll have no way of getting the powder into the hydra's eyes." Skylar shook her head, looking defeated for the first time.

"You know," said Aldwyn after a minute of silence, "I might not have telekinesis, but I'm pretty good at climbing things."

"Living things?" asked Skylar.

"I jumped on the back of a butcher once," said Aldwyn.

"Living things with seven heads that will try to kill you?" asked Skylar again.

"That would be new for me."

Gilbert looked pleadingly at the blue jay.

"Come on, admit it," he said. "We can't do this alone. We need Aldwyn's help."

"Fine," Skylar said after a short pause. "I don't really see any other option."

Skylar got to her feet and hobbled forwards. Gilbert hopped along with her. Aldwyn just stood there – did he hear her correctly?

"Well?" asked Skylar, turning back. "What are you waiting for?"

Aldwyn immediately ran up beside them. He had been accepted back into the fellowship. And this time, he would not have to pretend to have skills he didn't have. He only hoped that the talents he had acquired on the streets of Bridgetower would not fail him.

The land had taken on a golden glow and the sun was nearing the horizon as the familiars hurried to beat the approaching sunset. Aldwyn was certain that Queen Loranella was watching the sun too, waiting patiently for the last rays of light to disappear.

SIXTEEN

The Sunken Palace

Never before had a quick pace been of greater importance on their journey, and yet the familiars were moving slower than ever. Skylar had made a makeshift splint for her broken wing out of her satchel strap. Her injury forced the normally swift-flying bird to travel on foot. Aldwyn and Gilbert had considered racing ahead without her, but even though she was handicapped, they knew Skylar's illusions could mean the difference between victory and defeat in their battle against the hydra.

The three animals had left the banks of the Ebs behind and were now crossing a wasteland enshrouded in the mists churned up from the crashing waters of the Torentia Falls. The rays of the sinking sun created ever-changing patterns of light wherever you looked. The entire region seemed haunted. Aldwyn had the anxious feeling he used to get whenever he took a shortcut through Bridgetower's lone cemetery. The air was still and a terrible sadness seemed to cling to every blade of grass. They were following the remains of an ancient road, a two-cart-wide path of mud and pebbles, with wagon wheel tracks petrified in the ground like fossils.

As the sun crept closer to the horizon, the road suddenly ended. Ahead of them, the earth had been overturned, just as if it had been tilled by a gigantic plough. The thick mist over the land hid from view whatever lay beyond.

"This must be the edge of Mukrete," said Skylar, "the city in which the Old Palace of Vastia once stood. Before the curse."

"Not another curse," said Gilbert nervously.

"I'm afraid so. This one sank the Old Palace and all of Mukrete with it." Skylar picked up the pace again, and they walked onto the ravaged land and deeper into the mist.

"Nearly two centuries ago," continued Skylar, "King Brannfalk, the grandfather of Loranella's grandfather, ruled Vastia. According to the historical scrolls, he was hot-tempered and prideful and a lover of dragons. In fact, he kept seven of them in the Old Palace stables. He was so protective of his prized pets that he demanded they be guarded day and night, a job which fell to a one-eyed ogre, a creature said to have traded his second eye for the ability to cast magic.

"One morning the king came to check on the dragons and found that they were all missing. When questioned, the ogre insisted that he had locked the stables the night before and all seven had been safely inside. As nobody else had a key to the stables, the ogre was accused of stealing and eating them – an understandable claim, given the never-ending appetite of most ogres. Besides, when his sleeping quarters were inspected, a dragon's foot was discovered beneath his bed. Only the bones remained, the meat having been scraped clean off.

"The ogre pleaded his innocence, but to no avail: he was sentenced to death, but to the very end claimed that he had been framed. Just before the executioner's axe fell, the ogre used the magic he traded his eye for to place a curse on the king's palace and all that surrounded it.

"At the moment his head was severed from his body, the ground opened up, swallowing palace and town alike. Some escaped, but many were buried alive."

Aldwyn stepped more cautiously, aware that far beneath his paws lay a buried city, its buildings and streets encased in mud and dirt.

"Well, was the ogre innocent?" asked Gilbert.

"I'm getting there," said Skylar. "I haven't finished the story yet. Brannfalk was one of the survivors; he managed to escape the sinking castle by jumping off the balcony of the palace's highest tower. So did the Palace Wizard, who in his own desperate getaway dragged a chest containing his most precious research up the tower with him. But in his haste, it broke and spilled open, revealing severed dragon body parts, and eyes, teeth and talons. He was the one guilty of the dragon slayings, not the ogre whom he had framed.

"The Palace Wizard had experimented on the dragons in the hope of engineering an undefeatable dragon, obedient only to him, that would become his familiar. But his forbidden necromancy had been unsuccessful. In an attempt to hide his dark experiments, he poured the contents of his failed spells down the dungeon well. Little could he know that what he was unable to achieve over those few terrible nights, nature with its infinite patience would accomplish over the span of a hundred years. For there, in that well, the stew of all seven of the king's dragons eventually grew into the perfect dragon: the creature that we know today as the Hydra of Mukrete."

"Wait a second," said Gilbert, "you mean—?"

"That's right," replied Skylar. "It's the very dragon that has been guarding the Sunken Palace ever since."

Aldwyn's mind was racing. He remembered his alley days, when he was often outsized and outmatched. He always found a way to turn the odds in his favour, whether it was by his lightning quick reflexes, clever thinking, or just sheer guts. But would those skills be enough when fighting a seven-headed monster?

"So, Skylar," said Aldwyn. "Does this hydra have any weak spots? Something that might slow it down?"

"I know a little about the seven heads," she replied. "You see, Brannfalk had collected one dragon from each of the seven northern species. There's a fire-breather, fairly typical; a shrieker, whose wail has been known to cause madness if you're exposed to it for too long; a tunneller, whose spiked horns can bore through any mountain. You remember the acid spitter? We already know what *it* is capable of. And then there are the three really dangerous heads."

Aldwyn swallowed. The ones Skylar had already told them about seemed bad enough.

"The first of those is the hive dragon," continued Skylar. She seemed to take pleasure in describing their foe in detail. "Poisonous hornets live in its nostrils. The second is the black-tooth, whose bite causes instant death, so you should definitely avoid that one.

And the final head is the python strangler, whose forked tongue can squeeze the life out of a full-sized gundabeast."

"You didn't answer my question," Aldwyn interrupted her.

"Oh, I'm sorry. What was it again?"

"Any weak spots?" he reminded her.

"None that I know of."

Aldwyn's uneasiness grew.

"Don't worry," said Skylar. "I'll be casting illusions to help."

"What about me?" asked Gilbert. "What am I supposed to do?"

"You're going to be bait," she said.

Shortly afterwards, the mist began to lift and Aldwyn spotted a tower of stone jutting out of the ground like a giant mushroom, tilting ever-so-slightly.

"This must be the high tower of the Old Palace. The one Brannfalk escaped from," said Skylar. It was the only thing from all of Mukrete that had remained visible above the overturned earth.

Through an arched window, half above ground and

half below, Aldwyn could see a spiral staircase leading downward.

"Guys, over here," said Aldwyn. "It looks like a way in."

Aldwyn was the first to climb through, jumping down onto a marble step beneath the window. Skylar peered through the opening, assessing the distance of the drop.

"Gilbert, I could do with a little help," she said.

Gilbert supported her, lowering her down to the ground, and Aldwyn was there to ease the landing. Gilbert followed, hopping down beside them.

Aldwyn took one last look up through the window and could see a sliver of sky, the clouds now turning orange-pink, a sure sign that sunset was approaching. Before he turned back for the stairs, he could have sworn he saw a small flock of spyballs fly past outside.

"Come on," said Skylar. "We have to go a long way down. It says in the scrolls that the Old Palace's high tower reached twenty storeys into the sky. And who knows how deep the dungeon lies."

They began their twisting descent, making winding circles around the central stone pillar of the staircase.

The granite walls were remarkably well-preserved; the superior architecture had prevented even the slightest cracks in their surface. The windows had mud and earth pressed against them, revealing a cross-section of worm trails and mole tunnels. As the familiars moved lower, the air became stale and still. No breeze had passed through this tower for two hundred years. Their descent into the buried underground fortress was lit by steady flames coming from wall-mounted candleless holders. Skylar identified this wax- and wick-free magical device as Protho's Lights, named after the great magical inventor, Orachnis Protho.

"Hey, wait a minute," said Gilbert suddenly.

Aldwyn and Skylar turned back to him. The tree frog had stopped beneath an open window, standing beside a pile of dirt on the floor.

"That's great, Gilbert, but we've seen dirt before," said Aldwyn.

"No, look," said the tree frog as he picked up a gold-capped tube from the floor. "It's one of Marianne's pocket scrolls. It must have slipped out of her sleeping shirt."

"They're really here!" whispered Aldwyn to himself. The hope that they weren't too late washed over him.

Just then, he felt some pebbles fall on his shoulder. He glanced up at the window and saw a horde of giant earth mites scurry in from the dried soil outside. They were the size of grapes, with hard shells and six pointy legs. The ground-dwelling insects crawled down the side of the wall, moving quickly towards them. "What are they?" asked Aldwyn, with alarm in his voice.

"I don't know," replied Skylar.

Aldwyn and Gilbert both gave her a look of surprise.

"What? I don't know everything," she said, using her good wing to try to knock a couple of the bugs that had fallen onto her from her feathers.

"First vampire leeches, now this," said an exasperated Gilbert. "I'm really done for this time!"

Aldwyn tried to shake off the handful of bugs that had landed on his fur.

"Aldwyn, Gilbert, relax," said Skylar. "They're not biting."

They both stopped their flailing.

"They're not?" asked Gilbert.

"They're not," said Aldwyn.

"I think they're just looking for a warm place to nestle," she added.

Skylar reached into her pouch with her beak and removed some sage, juniper and nightshade. She tossed the components into the air and chanted.

"Send a flame from whence you came!"

A small female fire spirit materialised and the bugs immediately swarmed in the direction of the fairy's glowing form.

Aldwyn used his claw to pull one last hanger-on from his hind leg and dropped it on the ground. Skylar and Gilbert, now free and clear as well, were moving further down the steps, leaving the heat-seeking crawlers behind.

They headed deeper and deeper into the bowels of the Sunken Palace. Soon, they could hear haunting music. Around a bend at the end of the staircase, they found what appeared to be a banqueting chamber. Large sofas and chairs in one corner surrounded an enchanted harp playing a melancholy tune, as if a musical recital of some sort had taken place here long ago and never ended. One of the strings was out of key and every time it was plucked a flat note pierced the air. Crystal glasses with traces of wine and plates covered with quail bones were still left on the tables, abandoned in a rush when the ogre's curse had plunged the castle into the ground. Save for some cobwebs and dust, Aldwyn thought, this is what the place must have looked like two centuries ago.

He looked at the paintings on the walls. One seemed to be a portrait of King Brannfalk. His resemblance to Queen Loranella was unmistakable. Aldwyn's eyes then turned to the floor.

"Look, footprints."

Tracks in the dust led to a wooden door. The trio followed them onto the second-floor landing overlooking the great hall. Aldwyn stood in awe. Never before had he been inside a room so enormous. There were marble staircases on either side of the landing. Rows of columns supported the high domed ceiling, from which hung metal chandeliers holding Protho's Lights. The floor displayed a large tile-mosaic of King Brannfalk's face. Skylar had been right when she said he was prideful: this was vanity unchecked!

Two large archways connected to neighbouring rooms. Aldwyn could see that one was the throne room; the other he couldn't see into from where he was standing. Unlike the banqueting chamber they had passed through, the great hall appeared to have been ravaged by battle. The walls were singed where fire had baked tapestries to ash, and chunks of stone had been splintered as if by mighty blasts of energy. Heavy wooden furniture had been crushed and a table overturned. Dented suits of armour lined the wall. One of the stairway's marble banisters looked as if a large part of it had been melted away.

An ominous silence hovered over the place, broken only by the distant melody of the out-of-tune harp. As Aldwyn took his first steps down the stairs, he felt the ground move beneath his feet. He thought that the earth had given way and the castle was sinking even deeper. Either that, or – these were the footsteps of the seven-headed hydra.

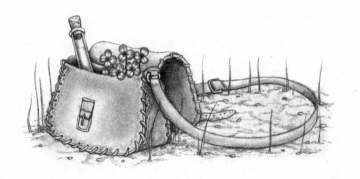

SEVENTEEN

The Hydra of Mukrete

Aldwyn didn't have to wait long to get his answer: in the throne room's archway, a single dragon-head appeared. Then another. Then a third and a fourth. Each a different size and colour. The last three heads came all together, along with the beast's giant body: smooth and green with jagged spikes on its tail. The Hydra of Mukrete stood thirty-feet tall and was nearly as long.

Aldwyn, Gilbert and Skylar froze in their tracks.

Nothing they'd been told prepared them for the fearsome monster now blocking their path.

"*Eeeeeeeiiiiiiiiiiiiii!*"

The high-pitched, eardrum-shattering wail came from the head of the shrieker. It had a long, beige speckled neck and an impossibly large mouth. Its cry alerted the other wandering heads to what it had just discovered. In a flash, fourteen malevolent dragon eyes were gazing at the familiars, who were holding their ears, attempting to block the shrieker's wail any way they could.

"Gilbert, the sleeping powder!" shouted Aldwyn over the deafening scream.

"What?" Aldwyn thought he heard Gilbert respond, but he wasn't quite sure.

"THE SLEEPING POWDER!" Aldwyn yelled, trying to be heard over the shrieker dragon.

Skylar was shouting too, gesturing frantically to Gilbert, who seemed both confused and terrified. The hydra was stomping closer – its thick, clawed feet dragging its heavy body across the floor at a worrying speed.

Aldwyn tried pantomime instead, cupping his

paws together and curling up to them as if pretending to sleep. He then shook his paw as if pouring something from a vial. Gilbert finally got the message and removed the glass container with its precious powder from Jack's pouch. Aldwyn took it in his teeth. The hydra had moved down the alley of columns right up to the staircase on which the familiars were still standing, but the shrieker took a breath, giving them a quick chance to talk.

"Gilbert and I will distract it from the ground," said Skylar to Aldwyn. "Good luck."

At that moment, a blast of fire hit the stone steps, landing right between Aldwyn and his two fellow familiars. He looked up to see that the blast had come from the red-eyed fire-breather. Its mouth was dripping steaming saliva. Skylar and Gilbert hurried down the staircase, drawing the fire-breather's attention away from Aldwyn. A trail of orange flames was nipping at their heels. Aldwyn sprinted upwards, hoping to climb high enough to jump on top of the beast. As he ran, the smallest of the seven heads opened its mouth and flipped up its tongue. A stream of yellow liquid shot towards

Aldwyn. When the discharge made contact with the marble, it began to eat away at it instantly. This was the acid spitter. Aldwyn had to leap from step to step as its venom burnt simmering holes in his path.

Aldwyn caught a glimpse of Skylar and Gilbert through the banisters as they reached the floor and sprinted towards the dented suits of armour standing against the wall. The head of the black-tooth, with hollowed out eyes and rows of rotting teeth, darted towards them. It might have swallowed both familiars whole had it not been for the shrieker's head, which was pulling the hydra in the other direction, straight for Aldwyn.

As the shrieker wailed again, Aldwyn jumped atop the narrow stone banister. The head came up alongside him, the inhuman noise getting louder the closer it got. But instead of running away, Aldwyn leaped onto its snout. He stuck one of his claws into the vial's cork stopper and tugged it out with a pop. The enraged head of the shrieker barely had time to react as Aldwyn pounced to its eye and tipped a dash of the alchemist's dark yellow sleeping powder into the socket.

Instantly, the shrieker's pupil dilated and the entire eye became glassy. The dragon fell silent – the first of the seven heads had fallen fast asleep. As the shrieker's neck began to go limp, Aldwyn dashed across it towards the hydra's main body, recorking the vial as he ran.

"That wasn't so bad," he said to himself, a little surprised, but also gaining confidence.

The feeling didn't last long, though. Out of the corner of his eye he spotted a pair of twisted horns rushing towards him – the horns of the tunneller dragon. He dodged them at the very last second, their spiked tips just grazing his fur. Before the tunneller could take a second stab at him, Aldwyn vaulted to the neighbouring neck of the acid spitter.

As the horns charged at him again, Aldwyn stood his ground, leaving himself a clear target for the tunneller's attack. He waited as the spiked tips rushed towards him, slicing through the air. Then, at the last moment, he vaulted upwards, wrapping his paws around the nearest chandelier. The tunneller couldn't stop the momentum of his charge and its horns pierced the underside of the acid-spitter's long neck, puncturing its salivary gland and sending a stream of acid gushing from the hole. The head of the spitter slammed to the ground, a flood of acid spreading across the floor.

Two down, thought Aldwyn as he pulled himself up to the relative safety of the hanging chandelier. From here, he could see that Skylar and Gilbert were hiding behind the suits of armour. Unfortunately, the fire breather was rapidly approaching them, shooting flames from its mouth. Aldwyn knew that his friends would be cooked if he didn't do something. He used his weight to swing the chandelier towards the head of the fire breather, whose breath had nearly melted through the plate-metal armour protecting Skylar and Gilbert. Aldwyn uncorked the vial of sleeping powder and sprinkled a dusting into the creature's red, beady eyes. The fire breather wheezed out one last puff of smoke before its neck collapsed into a snoring heap on the ground.

Gilbert and Skylar were no longer in danger of being singed, but now the wide-nosed head of the hive dragon was coming towards them. It let out a powerful snort – unleashing a swarm of black-and-yellow hornets. The stinging insects buzzed around the room, dipping and diving towards Gilbert and Skylar, who were forced to flee from behind the melted armour.

"Keep moving," yelled Skylar to Gilbert. "If you stop they'll cluster around you. And believe me, you don't want to be stung by even one. Their toxins can kill a grown man instantly."

Frog and bird hopped along the giant mosaic. The pool of acid from the spitter was spreading, dissolving the floor and half of King Brannfalk's mosaic face. From his perch atop the chandelier, Aldwyn could see through the rapidly growing hole in the floor. Beneath the great hall was the Palace Vault and all its treasures: gold coins piled high, crystal sceptres, jewel-encrusted crowns and bronze bathtubs filled with gems.

Just then, from behind Aldwyn, the head of the black-tooth lashed out with a vicious bite. It snapped the chain of the chandelier, sending Aldwyn and Protho's Lights crashing to the floor below. Skylar and Gilbert were running for their lives from the horde of nostril wasps, but the fallen chandelier, with a dazed Aldwyn sitting on it, now blocked their path of escape. Aldwyn watched as one of the deadly insects landed on Gilbert's shoulder and inserted its sting into the tree frog's slimy skin.

"Gilbert, NO!" exclaimed Skylar, who saw what was happening as well. She reached for a candlestick holder from the chandelier with her claw and waved one of Protho's Lights in the air, momentarily warding off the killer insects.

Gilbert looked down at the black hornet prong embedded in his arm. "Tell Marianne I tried my best," he said.

"Just hang in there," said Aldwyn, trying to comfort Gilbert.

Skylar continued to hold back the hornets with the glowing blue torch. She turned and noticed that Gilbert looked no worse than before.

"Gilbert, aren't you in excruciating pain?" she asked.

"As a matter of fact, I'm not."

"You should be dead by now," she added.

Gilbert perked up considerably at this good piece of news.

"That's strange. Now that you mention it, I don't feel anything."

"You must be immune to their poison," said Skylar.

"I guess that makes sense," he replied. "Mosquitoes, stinging beetles, poisonous bees: none of them can hurt frogs. In fact, we like to think of them less as enemies and more as appetisers." A grin crossed his face. "Please allow me."

Skylar lowered the flame and with lightning speed Gilbert's pink tongue began to dart here and there, plucking the stinging hornets out of the air and flinging them down his gullet. He was taking them out in bunches!

The hornets were no longer a threat to the familiars, but the tunneller had twisted past the other heads and was now bearing down in an attempt to skewer Aldwyn again. He scampered away as the horned dragon-head chased him across the floor. Aldwyn looked to his right and there was... Aldwyn? A cat just like himself was running alongside him. He first thought this was some kind of delayed brain trauma from his fall on the chandelier, but then looked over his shoulder and saw Skylar with trembling wing outstretched before her. This was no side effect of a head injury; it was another of Skylar's illusions.

The duplicate Aldwyn broke off from the real one and the tunneller took the bait, following not the flesh-and-blood cat, but the fake one. The illusion of Aldwyn stopped before one of the columns and just stood there, making faces at the dragon. Aldwyn watched as the tunneller tried to gouge it, but instead the horns went straight through the air, burying themselves in the stone pillar. The head strained, trying to pull itself free, but before it could, Aldwyn poured a healthy dose of sleeping powder into one of its eyes. The tunneller sank instantly into a deep sleep. Aldwyn corked the vial and turned back to Skylar.

"Thanks, Sky—"

Shlap!

A mighty blow from the long, twisting tongue of the python strangler smacked Aldwyn against the ground and flung the glass tube of powder along the tiled floor, bumping and bouncing as it headed straight for the gaping hole formed by the acid spitter's saliva.

Aldwyn couldn't dwell on the shock of pain coursing through his body from the wallop; he was already running again to retrieve the powder. He dived for the vial and swiped it away from the edge just as the acid dissolved the floor beneath it. He gripped it securely between his teeth and turned around to find the hive dragon flaring his nostrils at him. With a ferocious snort, it released another cloud of poisonous insects. Aldwyn was trapped between the swarm heading towards him and the disappearing ground behind him. He braced himself for the attack, but before the hornets could strike, Gilbert leaped into the fray again, snaring dozens at a time. Wielding his tongue with a warrior's skill that would have made his Daku relatives proud, the tree frog provided cover for Aldwyn, allowing him to jump onto the hive dragon's lowered head. He sprinkled powder in its eye and it was asleep on the floor before Aldwyn even had time to recork the vial.

Aldwyn surveyed the scene, planning his next move. The hydra was moving more slowly now, dragging the weight of five unconscious necks and heads behind it. Gilbert was catching the last of the hornets, while Skylar had cast an illusion of a swift-winged condor that circled around the head of the black-toothed dragon. And the python strangler... the python strangler was in the process of wrapping its forked tongue around Aldwyn's hind legs!

Aldwyn was jerked off the nose of the hive dragon and into the air, the dragon squeezing tight as Aldwyn was pulled towards the gaping mouth of the python strangler.

"Gilbert, Skylar, help!" shouted Aldwyn through clenched teeth, still gripping the vial.

But Gilbert could only watch helplessly. Skylar redirected the illusory condor to soar past the strangler's nose, but it didn't work. Aldwyn could already smell the foul stench of the dragon head's warm breath. So this was the end. Aldwyn's adventure across Vastia would go no further. He comforted himself with the thought that at least Skylar and Gilbert might have a chance to save Jack,

Marianne and Dalton should he die here.

Thwoop!

The grip of the python strangler's tongue loosened and Aldwyn dropped to the ground. He looked up and saw an arrow-like projectile stuck in the fleshy pink muscle. A second bolt struck the tongue. Aldwyn spun around to see who was responsible for saving him. There, standing on the second floor landing with crossbow in hand, was – Grimslade!

"That bounty is mine, beast," called the cloaked hunter to the dragon.

Aldwyn could not believe that his old adversary had returned yet again. He must have pulled himself up from the Bridge of Betrayal and tracked the familiars here. And while normally Grimslade was the last person Aldwyn ever wanted to see, right now he was more than welcome.

Grimslade fired off another round from his crossbow, sending the strangler into a thrashing fit of pain. As the head brushed against the floor, attempting to dislodge one of Grimslade's bolts from its cheek, Aldwyn pounced upon its coarse scales. The hydra's head was whipping violently back and forth, making it a dangerous climb to the eyes, but Aldwyn clung on. Once within range, he sprinkled the powder into the monster's tear duct. The skull came crashing down with a bang.

Only the black-toothed head remained awake on the hydra, and it wasn't going to let them pass without a fight. Its neck was already wiring its way in the direction of Grimslade. The bounty hunter took aim and sent two more projectiles at its lower jaw. But its skin must have been thicker than that of the python strangler's because the bolts merely bounced off when they made contact. With incredible speed, it bared its rotting fangs and thrust forwards. Grimslade dropped his bow and pulled out the noose stick, shoving it into the wide open mouth lunging towards him. He pressed the blunt end of the pole up against the roof of its mouth, keeping it locked in place as the decaying teeth struggled to bite down.

Aldwyn had taken to the stairs, leaping them two at a time as he raced to put the final head to sleep, while the stalemate between man and hydra continued.

"Come now," taunted Grimslade. "I've seen garden snakes put up a better fight than this."

The black-tooth snapped down on the stick, splintering it like a toothpick. Grimslade, left with a tiny shard of wood in his hand, backed away as the hydra's head got ready to strike. Aldwyn sprinted to the top of the staircase and ran straight up Grimslade's back, using the bounty hunter as a springboard to launch himself onto the snout of the black tooth. Before it could deliver its deathly blow, Aldwyn tipped the vial, pouring the last remaining grains into its eye. Its mighty head sank limply onto the banister, and Aldwyn found himself face to face with Grimslade.

"Much obliged, cat," said the bounty hunter. "But I still plan on turning you and your companions in." As Grimslade bent down to grab his crossbow, Aldwyn noticed a sprinkling of yellow-coloured powder on the fur of his front leg. He blew the fine particles straight into Grimslade's face, and the bounty hunter collapsed, his head falling against the nose of the black-toothed dragon.

Aldwyn ran down the steps to join Skylar and Gilbert.

"We need to find that dungeon," he said, hoping that the sun had not set yet.

"Most palaces have secret passageways from the throne room," said Skylar. "This way."

She led them out of the great hall, beneath one of the archways and into a room filled with velvet curtains and more portraits of King Brannfalk. A large wooden throne sat in the centre of the room, its high back and headrest carved into the shape of a blossoming tree. Aldwyn recognised it from the stamp on the bricks of the Bridge of Betrayal.

"I owe you an apology," said Skylar to Aldwyn. "It seems I've overestimated the value of magic. Your display back there was worthy of any of the greatest wizards of yore, human or animal. Kalstaff would have been proud of you. And so am I."

Aldwyn's eyes welled up. He could think of no greater compliment. This was the most gratifying moment of his young life.

"Thank you. And apology accepted."

Beyond the throne, a rug had been pulled aside revealing an open trapdoor with a sloping stone corridor that led downwards. The familiars quickly crossed the room and entered.

The magic candle-holders were dimmer inside the corridor and it was difficult to see past each bend. Aldwyn heard footsteps and turned to his friends.

"Over there," he said, gesturing to a shadow moving across the wall.

The animals braced themselves for another confrontation.

"Oh, thank goodness you're here," called out a soft, timid voice.

Then, into the light bounced a small, grey rabbit.

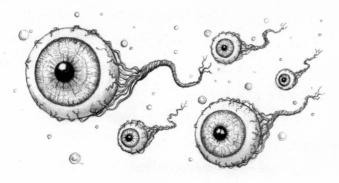

EIGHTEEN

Paksahara

Aldwyn recognised her immediately from the picture in Kalstaff's cottage. It was Paksahara, Queen Loranella's familiar.

"Thank goodness you're here," Paksahara repeated, with tears of gratitude. "The queen has gone mad. She's intentionally sabotaging the order and safety of Vastia and its people, making it defenceless to an invasion from the outside lands. I've tried to reason with her, but she won't listen. I'm just fortunate to have escaped before any harm was done to me."

"Where is she now?" asked Skylar.

"She's gone back to the New Palace," replied Paksahara, "but she will return at sundown, when Kalstaff's protective spell expires, to eliminate the only thing standing in the way of her plan. We must save the wizards at once."

"Are they hurt?" asked Skylar.

"No, Kalstaff's spell has kept them from harm, but not for much longer. Quickly, follow me!"

They began to move down the tunnel, deeper into the belly of the palace. They passed cells now empty but with claw marks on the walls and fang marks on the bars. Aldwyn realised this hadn't been a dungeon solely for Vastia's most dangerous criminals of yesteryear, but a gaol where magical beasts and animals had been imprisoned as well.

"How have you made it so far unaided by wizards?" Paksahara asked the three familiars.

"We didn't think it was possible at first, either," said Skylar. "But maybe we animals have more power than humans have led us to believe."

"That's impossible," replied Paksahara.

"We've seen things that might change your mind," said Skylar.

Their descent became steeper and steeper as Paksahara led them further, her floppy ears and fluffy bunny tail bouncing with every step.

"But clearly you are devoted to your loyals to have risked so much."

"I would do anything for Marianne," said Gilbert.

"And I for Dalton," said Skylar.

"What about you?" Paksahara asked, turning to Aldwyn.

"I'm not even a true familiar," he said. "I have no magical abilities. Yet I take great pride in serving Jack."

"It sounds like all of you would give your lives for these wizards," said Paksahara. "I felt that way, too, about the queen," she added with a sad twitch of her nose.

Just then, a voice in the distance cried out.

"Help, somebody! Please!"

Aldwyn's heart jumped upon hearing the voice.

"We're coming, Jack!" shouted Aldwyn, and he started racing towards him. Gilbert began jumping like mad too, and Skylar was half fluttering, no longer thinking about the pain in her wing.

"It's just up ahead," said Paksahara, keeping pace beside them, hopping effortlessly on her long legs.

"Hang in there, Marianne!" called Gilbert.

Gilbert had tears in his eyes when they entered the circular dungeon chamber. On the walls Aldwyn spied swords and shields. Taming whips and muzzles gave more evidence that animals had once been imprisoned here too. The floor was cold, wet and had claw marks scraped into the stone. The damp room had no cobwebs — even spiders seemed to be avoiding this dank pit. And there on the far wall were Jack, Marianne and Dalton. Still dressed in the sleeping linens they were kidnapped in, they were shackled by their wrists, held fast by iron dispeller chains. A rusty bucket half-filled with water rested at their feet. Kalstaff's protective forcefields were not glowing strongly any more; they appeared on the verge of disappearing.

Gilbert jumped to Marianne's side, clutching her leg; Skylar hobbled to Dalton, nuzzling her head against him; and Aldwyn ran to Jack as if they had been companions always.

"I knew you'd come for us," said Jack, wanting to embrace Aldwyn but unable to, his arms held overhead by the bonds. "I knew it."

"I have so much to tell you," said Aldwyn, burying his whiskers into Jack's shin. "I don't even know where to begin."

"The queen left just a short while ago," said Dalton. "You must free us from these chains. We can't cast spells while we're shackled."

"I know the spell that will conjure a force key to unlock them," said Paksahara. "But I need the strength of you all. Familiars, stand before me and face your loyals. I will channel all of our powers together. You, too, Aldwyn."

Aldwyn, Skylar and Gilbert backed away from the wizards and lined up in front of Paksahara.

"What did she say?" asked Jack.

"She's going to summon a force key," said Aldwyn.

"I didn't know rabbits were capable of such powerful magic," said Jack.

"Tell the boy I'm no rabbit," said Paksahara, sounding rather insulted. "Rabbits are for lowly cider-house magicians. I am a hare."

The distinction really didn't seem that important to Aldwyn; what mattered was freeing Jack and escaping this dungeon at once.

Paksahara held up her furry grey paws and began chanting.

"*Dovolajen oknamut supentin!*"

"Hare?" said Gilbert quietly to himself.

Aldwyn turned to look at him.

"Hare," the tree frog repeated.

"*Zi po ukoteni wysove*," Paksahara continued to incant, her paws now glowing green.

"Grey hare," said Gilbert, still working out some kind of puzzle in his head. "Grey haired. *Grey hare witch!*"

"*Ekonpiske v prave*," said Paksahara, her voice rising.

Energy was crackling at the tips of her paws.

"Noooooo!" screamed Gilbert. He leaped, shoving Aldwyn and Skylar out of the way just as a deadly bolt of energy shot towards them from Paksahara's paws. It hit the wall, leaving a gaping hole.

"It was you," shouted Gilbert, pointing to Paksahara. "You were the witch all along."

"What are you talking about?" asked Skylar.

"My puddle viewing. Don't you see? *She*'s the grey hare witch. Not Agdaleen."

Paksahara stood across from them, smoke drifting from her paws, the pinks of her eyes glistening evilly.

"I don't understand," said Skylar. "You're working with the queen?"

"Oh, no," replied Paksahara, her once innocent voice now flat and cold. "The queen has been imprisoned for many moons, trapped as a hare in a cage in the palace. Perhaps you're unaware, but my magical talent, my innate ability, is..."

"Shapeshifting," said Skylar.

"What's she saying?" asked Dalton. "Would somebody please tell us what's going on?"

Paksahara flicked her paw at the children and an airy cloud surrounded them. Dalton opened his mouth to speak again, but no sound came out. The three young wizards had been silenced by some kind of spell.

"Animals have served man for far too long," continued Paksahara. "I have seen the paintings on the walls of the Kailasa caves. We once ruled this land, until the humans erased our proud history. It's time humans were caged and put on leashes. It's time for wizards to serve familiars again, and for a four-legged creature to sit on throne of Vastia... Me."

Aldwyn was stunned. *She is the enemy responsible for Kalstaff's death and all the misery that had followed? An animal? A familiar?*

"These young wizards, they're not a threat to you," Skylar tried to reason with her. "Let them go."

"Don't try to fool me, stupid bird. I have seen the three stars in the sky fall over Stone Runlet," said Paksahara. "A prophecy that three young spellcasters would defeat me. They have to die. First, however, I'll take great pleasure in killing the three of you."

She raised her forelegs in the air.

"*Ekonpiske v prave,*" the hare incanted.

Two balls of lightning formed in her paws and she reached towards Aldwyn, Gilbert and Skylar. The double blast of energy cut through the air, heading directly for them. There was no time to move and nowhere to run. But before the familiars were struck, one of the metal shields hanging on the wall flew from its rack and blocked Paksahara's attack. The bursts of lightning sparked then fizzled upon contact with the steel plating of the shield.

Skylar and Gilbert turned to Aldwyn as the circle of armour continued to float between them and the grey hare.

"Aldwyn? What's going on?" asked Gilbert.

"I have no idea," he replied, just as confused as his fellow familiars. Aldwyn's head was dizzy with questions: how had the shield moved through the air on its own? Had it been his doing? Did he have telekinetic powers after all?

A loud crack rang out as the shield exploded into hot metal shards, obliterated by another of Paksahara's lightning bolts. The familiars scrambled, running off in three different directions.

The familiars' hope had been to divide and conquer, but Paksahara had no trouble attacking in three directions at the same time. She extended a paw towards Gilbert and he was immediately lifted off his feet, as if the air itself was holding him up by his throat. Paksahara then thrust her other paw at Aldwyn, sending a barrage of ruby needles flying like darts across the room. He made a running dive and managed to dodge all but one, which grazed his left hind leg.

"There's nowhere to hide," said Paksahara. "I'm going to send you all to the Tomorrowlife, just like I did Kalstaff."

With a flick of her tail, she invoked a gust of wind that engulfed Skylar in its powerful swirl before flinging her into the wall.

Although Aldwyn felt a sharp, jabbing pain every time his pierced leg touched the ground, he kept moving while his mind tried to think. Could he actually move things with his mind? There was only one way to find out: he would try again.

As Gilbert struggled, still caught in the stranglehold of Paksahara's spell, Aldwyn focused on the rusty bucket of water. He had no idea how telekinesis worked, but concentrating really hard and focusing his mind seemed a logical place to start. *Lift. Lift. Lift. Lif—*

And just like that, the bucket was floating up off the ground. Now what?

Aldwyn didn't have a chance to experiment with his newly discovered talent any further: Paksahara fired a surge of purple energy at the bucket that destroyed it in a flash. Though Aldwyn's first deliberate attempt at magic ended quickly, it had been enough to distract Paksahara, who had released her stranglehold on Gilbert. The tree frog landed on the ground, clutching his throat and taking big, heavy breaths.

"So you have magic after all, cat," said Paksahara. "It's a shame you won't have time to learn how to use it."

She narrowed her pink eyes viciously, about to cast another spell. Then three popping sounds could be heard – Kalstaff's protective bubbles had burst. Jack, Marianne and Dalton remained chained to the wall, and now they were no longer immune to Paksahara's evil magic.

"Now, there will be nothing to stand in my way," said Paksahara.

From her paws, she unleashed a spear of white light aimed directly at Jack's chest. Aldwyn could only watch in horror as it struck his loyal – but rather than searing a hole straight through his body, the beam bounced back towards Paksahara. She was knocked across the room, her grey fur singed.

Aldwyn at first couldn't understand what had just happened. Then he saw Skylar, who had recovered from Paksahara's attack and was holding up a trembling wing. As she lowered it, the bubbles returned. Aldwyn realised that Skylar had cast a sneaky illusion, one that made it seem as if the protective shells had gone when in reality they had still been there. While the trick had nearly made Aldwyn's heart stop, it had given them their first successful strike against their enemy.

But Paksahara was far from finished. She rose to her feet, more hateful than before.

"Very clever," said Paksahara. "But illusions won't save you."

"Don't do this," implored Aldwyn. Out of the corner of his eye, he'd seen Gilbert remove Marianne's pocket scroll from the gold-capped tube in his pouch. It seemed he was looking for a spell. "I'm sure Queen Loranella could find a place for you on the Council," he continued, trying to stall her. "Think about it, animal and human working together. It could be the start of a new Vastia."

"The new Vastia I imagine has no place for those

who walk on two legs," said Paksahara.

At which point Gilbert triumphantly shouted, "*Convulsare minimosus!*"

Paksahara only shook her head.

"And what powerful magic does that spell con – *hic* – jure?" she asked, putting a paw to her chest.

"Hiccups?" said Aldwyn in disbelief to Gilbert. "That's what you had me stalling her for?"

"It was between that and burping," said Gilbert. "This is a practical joke scroll."

"You three are pa – *hic* – thetic," said Paksahara. She held her breath for a moment, and when she exhaled the diversion was gone as quickly as it had come. "Now, where was I?"

Just then, a *whooshing* sound could be heard behind them – the third day's sun had set, and the bubbles protecting the young wizards had evaporated for real this time.

"And about time, too," said Paksahara. "Step out of my way. In exchange, I promise I will kill your loyals painlessly."

Aldwyn stared at the wall of beast-taming weapons, but he couldn't clear his mind fast enough. Too many thoughts were swimming in his head for him to focus.

"Three times this must be said," incanted Paksahara, "and one alive will soon be dead." Her attention turned to the wizards, her eyes landing coldly on Dalton. "Shrivel and wither."

Aldwyn closed his eyes and willed the whip off the equipment rack. The brown leather strap wobbled through the air and was immediately dispatched with a fireball from Paksahara's free hand.

"Shrivel and wither," she said, finishing the second refrain.

Aldwyn knew she only had one more incantation left. He had to stop her before those three words spilled from her mouth.

"Shrivel..."

Aldwyn focused on the two swords mounted on the wall rack. He concentrated mightily and they started to rattle.

"...and..." continued Paksahara

The swords lifted from the wall and hovered in the air. Then a shock of electricity slammed Aldwyn off his feet. Paksahara had shot off another deadly bolt, breaking his mental grip and causing the weapons to crash to the ground.

"...wither!" Paksahara said triumphantly, completing the spell.

A thin pulse of blood-red energy fired out from her paw, slicing through the air straight for Dalton's heart. Aldwyn looked up from the floor to see Skylar flying upwards, broken wing pumping as fast as it could, to intercept the deadly attack. Paksahara's death spell made contact with the blue jay, felling her instantly. Dalton opened his mouth to scream, but no words came out. He was still muted by the silencing spell. Aldwyn's heart twisted in a knot. Gilbert seemed frozen in a total state of shock.

"A loyal familiar to the end," sniggered Paksahara. Her stare returned to the three young wizards. Her eyes homed in on Dalton once more. "Let's try this again. Shrivel and wither, shrivel and wither..." she incanted.

At this moment, the swords lifted off the ground and with a flash of silver flew across the room, pinning Paksahara to the ground.

"Ahhhh!" she wailed.

The two blades had crisscrossed in the air, then buried themselves deep into the stone floor, trapping the hare beneath.

"Do you really think your magic is a match for mine?" she asked, struggling to pull herself free.

Aldwyn wouldn't have thought so himself until a moment ago, but the power and swiftness of his telekinetic blow seemed to indicate otherwise.

"*Dovolajen oknamut supen*—" said Paksahara, with venom in her voice.

But before she could get her spell out, the muzzle that had been hanging on the wall was wrapped around her mouth. It moved so fast she didn't even see it coming. Her vengeful words were muffled as the leather bindings clamped her jaw shut.

"The queen will decide what to do with you," said Aldwyn.

Paksahara continued to flail, her pink eyes staring hatefully through the leather bands of the face guard.

Aldwyn and Gilbert ran over to Skylar's side. She lay there motionless.

"It's not fair," cried Gilbert. "She was my best friend."

"I know," said Aldwyn, putting a comforting paw on the tree frog's shoulder. "I know."

Then, miraculously, Skylar's wing began to move, and the blue jay sat up, looking confused. "I don't understand," she said. "How am I still alive? Life draining spells never fail to kill."

Aldwyn noticed that Skylar's pouch was steaming, a cooking odour emanating from within. He opened it up and out tumbled one of the white earth bugs, shrivelled and lifeless. The unlucky insect must have crawled in during the incident on the staircase and had become the unintended recipient of Paksahara's withering spell.

The three familiars couldn't help but smile at this stroke of good luck.

"What happened to Paksahara?" asked Skylar.

"She's pinned down over there," said Aldwyn.

But when he gestured across the room, the hare was no longer there. Instead, Aldwyn caught sight of a mud lizard scurrying away through a small hole in the wall. Paksahara had shapeshifted, and before any of them could react, she had disappeared.

"She's gone," said Skylar.

"Never mind, she'll be dealt with later," said Gilbert. "Let's free our loyals."

The familiars turned to Jack, Marianne and Dalton, whose mouths were moving with great excitement, though still no words were heard. Aldwyn stared at the bolts on the dispeller chains and his mind did the rest. He could hear clicking sounds as the gears inside the locks aligned. Then each one snapped open, releasing their loyals from the shackles. Aldwyn felt Jack's arms around him, clutching him tightly. He let out a purr as Jack stroked his fur, his tail curling happily.

Paksahara's silencing spell had yet to disappear, but once it did, they would have a lot of catching up to do.

NINETEEN

The Prophesised Three

Jack and Aldwyn were walking through the walled courtyard of the New Palace in Bronzhaven. A flag billowed from a pole overhead. With every flap of the wind, the canvas changed colour, showing a different coat of arms from Vastia's many cities, including Bridgetower's double-headed eagle with a bow and arrow in one talon and a wand in the other. Jack, bathed and dressed in a clean tunic and leggings, crossed a tiny arched bridge accompanied by a freshly brushed Aldwyn. They came to sit on a patch of moss beside a rock garden. Long, golden eels swam peacefully in the neighbouring pond.

It was hard to believe that only three days ago the familiars and their loyals had been reunited. They had left the Sunken Palace, sneaking past the sleeping hydra and Grimslade, who was still snuggled up to the head of the black-tooth. Then, under the light of the moon, they left behind the buried city of Mukrete and travelled to the hillside manor of Sorceress Edna, confident they could trust Kalstaff's fellow teacher of young wizards. Fortunately, she had just returned from one of her fieldtrips beyond the Borderlands. After listening to Dalton recount their story, Edna took it upon herself to secretly enter the palace and return Loranella to her rightful state, reversing the shapeshifting spell that had turned her into a hare. Once the queen was herself again, she had welcomed the young wizards and their familiars with open arms.

"Aldwyn, look," said Jack as he held his palm face down to the ground. "*Extollo!*" he commanded.

A fist-sized stone rose from the garden and levitated in the air.

"Wow, that's amazing," said Aldwyn.

"Now you try," said Jack.

Aldwyn channelled his energy and made ten rocks lift up from the pond and spin around in circles like heavenly bodies orbiting a star.

"You're going to have to teach me how to do that," said Jack, impressed.

Aldwyn let the stones fall back into the water. He was still marvelling at his new-found ability as well. He was a telekinetic cat, and that could mean only one thing: that his birthplace was, in fact, Maidenmere. He had been thinking a lot about his recurring dreams, and the pieces were starting to fit together: a small kitten on a bed of twigs, travelling down a river, to later wash up before a wall of white. Were those the outside walls of Bridgetower? It certainly would have made sense. He had been born in Maidenmere and abandoned, cast off from his home. But why, he wondered. And that female voice he heard in his dreams, could it be his mother's? What reason would she have had to rid herself of him? One mystery solved had opened up countless others.

"I still can't believe you fought a cave troll all by yourselves," said Jack, smiling. "How big was it again?"

"Before or after Gilbert accidentally gave it the colossus sap?"

"After."

"Big," said Aldwyn. "Really big."

Jack's eyes lit up. The only thing that would have made these amazing adventures better, Aldwyn thought, was if he and his loyal had shared them together.

From across the courtyard, Aldwyn could see Marianne and Dalton heading towards the rock garden. Skylar and Gilbert were right by their side. Skylar's wing was almost completely mended, thanks to the raven healer kept by the Royal Cleric, and Gilbert appeared relaxed; fresh from a bath in the palace's seaweed springs. Scribius, now polished and clean, glided along the ground behind them, making happy swirls as he followed in their path.

"I seem to recall the only one who didn't cry was me," said Marianne as she chased behind Dalton.

"I already told you, I'm allergic to dungeon mould."

"It's OK, I was scared too," she said, reaching out to touch him. "Oh, there you are," she continued, spotting her younger brother and Aldwyn. "We were wondering where the two of you had gone."

"We were just out here practising our magic," said Jack.

"Did you see the wishing web over by the everwillow tree?" asked Dalton.

"No, we must have walked right past it," said Jack, who was already leaping off the rock and running towards it.

"Careful!" called out Marianne. "You don't want to wish on the wrong spider."

Skylar and Gilbert went over to Aldwyn.

"You missed all the fun," said Skylar. "Sorceress Edna gave us a tour of the queen's library."

"I don't know if I would call it fun," said Gilbert. "Unless your idea of a good time is having excerpts from the botanical diaries of Phineus Pharkum read to you." Gilbert's eyes turned to the pond. "Oooh, are those golden eels?"

Aldwyn smiled. He wasn't really paying all that much attention, his mind elsewhere, still racing with questions.

"Skylar, can I ask you something?"

"Fire away," she replied.

"Why did these powers only come to me now? And so suddenly? I still don't understand."

"Ofttimes, a familiar's talent does not reveal itself until their loyal is in great peril," explained Skylar.

Aldwyn thought about Jack and how close Paksahara was to killing him. At the moment when everything seemed to be lost his powers of telekinesis had awakened.

"Or maybe there was something else at work," added Skylar. "Something we've yet to comprehend."

Aldwyn decided to ponder this mystery another time. He noticed Gilbert staring intently into the pond and wondered how fascinating those golden eels could really be. He walked up beside him and glanced into the water to see that Gilbert was having a puddle viewing. There on the shimmering surface of the pool was an image from Daku: Gilbert's dad stood alone in the Quag placing a valour staff into the ground. On its side was Gilbert's symbol, a circle with a star inside it. Gilbert beamed with pride.

Aldwyn smiled before stepping away, not wanting to intrude on his friend's personal moment of triumph.

"You can't make me tell," squealed Jack, as he ran back from the wishing web towards the rock garden, trying to avoid Marianne's tickling fingers. "If I do, it won't come true."

"Oh, come on," she urged. "Don't be so superstitious."

Dalton coughed noisily, and brother and sister fell silent at once. Queen Loranella, the real Queen Loranella, was approaching from the palace. She wore a long, golden gown and a thin crown on her white, shoulder-length hair. While she looked identical to the impostor Loranella that Paksahara had shape-shifted into during the battle at Stone Runlet, this queen didn't walk with the same arrogance.

"Hello, young wizards, familiars," she said formally but not without kindness. "I hope you have recovered from your adventures."

"Yes, Your Majesty, we have," said Dalton, speaking for all of them.

"Walk with me," said the queen, as she began to stroll through the courtyard towards the far garden wall.

Wizards and familiars walked alongside her.

"Once again, you have my thanks and the gratitude of all of Vastia," said Loranella. "Unfortunately, Paksahara remains at large, and she is clever, frightfully so. She stole from me a very powerful bracelet that belonged to my ancestor King Brannfalk. Its possessor can summon the Shifting Fortress, a secret stronghold that never appears in the same location twice. A spell cast from within those walls can affect all of Vastia. It is from where I conjure the enchanted fences, weather binding spells and other protective spells that have kept our lands safe for so long. One can only wonder what kind of darkness and destruction Paksahara hopes to rain down on the land from its highest tower. She must be stopped."

The queen walked across a stone path towards a bas-relief chiselled into the wall. The wizards and their animal companions joined her to see the carved image depicting a young Kalstaff, Loranella and Mountain Alchemist standing beneath three twisting stars shooting across the sky.

"Sixty years ago, we were the prophesised three," said the queen.

Aldwyn looked up at the three legendary figures: Kalstaff, the mentor he had known all too briefly; the Mountain Alchemist, who had become their reluctant ally; and Loranella, whom they had first falsely seen as an enemy but had, in fact, always been a friend.

"Together, we fulfilled our destiny," she added. "Now three young spellcasters from Stone Runlet are called upon to take our place."

Aldwyn, Skylar and Gilbert turned to their loyals, bursting with pride to be standing at their sides. Skylar held her head particularly high.

"We are honoured to carry on your legacies," Dalton said.

"That's very noble of you, Dalton," said the queen. "But you, Marianne and Jack are not the three chosen by the Heavens to protect Vastia. Paksahara made the same mistake when she assumed so."

The queen turned to the familiars.

"It is you: Aldwyn, Skylar and Gilbert. You are the prophesised three."

Jack turned to his magical companion with a new sense of awe and wonder.

Aldwyn couldn't believe what he had just heard. The fate of the entire land had been entrusted to him and his fellow familiars. His whiskers began to tingle, not for fish guts or chicken gizzards, like they had in the past. No, now they were tingling because he was hungry for something else – his next adventure.